Village Girls
BETH

Paula George

Village Girls
Beth

ISBN: 978-1-291-93645-2

A big 'Thank you,' to Edna, for all her help and encouragement.

Chapter 1

Bradfield Wick was a beautiful and peaceful village tucked away in a corner of the Cotswolds. The world seemed to have forgotten that it had ever been created. Outside influences were few and far between even in the first quarter of the twentieth century. The village cross, memorial of the Boer Wars, and more recently that terrible Great War which had robbed them of almost half a generation of men folk, was never allowed to stand in unkempt grass. The seat nearby was polished and cared for like the heirloom it was.

None of the houses were modern in design. Most were thatched cottages, like The Briary, home of John Gregory the local bobby, Briary Cottage, where Beth Riche lived, and Briary End, last in the row, and thankful retreat of the Haily family. Neil Haily was a teacher at the local school.

Just beyond the village lay the red brick mansion of Gannilea, home of Joel and Harriet Meekham. Along a narrow lane on the Gannilea estate stood a row of cottages. Harriet had gifted one to Chet Harding, her stable hand. Another had been bought by pianist Adair Stevens, while a young couple by the name of Freeman had the third. Sam Freeman had been crippled in the war and even though he had an award for his bravery he was finding it difficult to get work.

The last cottage had seen a lot of activity in the past months. A Tea Room had been opened in the nearby town and several villagers had remarked on how nice it was there. Harriet Meekham had decided that the villagers deserved a Tea Room of their own, and had brought in the builders to convert the empty cottage.

Now 'The Village Tea Room,' was ready to open its doors and do business. Much to Harriet's surprise something special was expected for the opening.

"They 'ad the mayor open the one in town," Chet informed her. "There was a posh orchestra playin' and fancy food. They even asked Lady Wilmore to come and make a speech."

"And did she?" Harriet had no liking for the lady, but was well aware of her place in the community.

"Yeah, and a more borin' speech I've never 'eard."

"Oh dear." The owner of The Village Tea Room sighed heavily. "I thought that all I would have to do was open the door and people would come in. I gave no thought to a Grand Opening."

"Suppose you got a few people together and 'ad a talk about it. Someone might 'ave some ideas."

"Yes," Harriet agreed ruefully, "I hope they might, because I haven't a clue. I am most certainly not going to ask Lady Wilmore, and the mayor is conceited enough without any encouragement."

Chet scratched thoughtfully at the hay littering the stable floor, watched lazily from his place on a nearby bale by the pale ginger stable cat, his darker, sleeker brother crouching nearby in hope of seeing a disturbed mouse. "You 'ave got something the town 'asn't," the young man said at last.

"Have I?" Harriet was intrigued.

"Yeah, you got an international pianist next door. Wonder 'ow that would go down?"

"Yes, I have, haven't I." Harriet lifted her head and smiled. "You really are a clever young man."

So it was that Harriet Meekham called a meeting of friends and neighbours one week before the day on which she expected to open for business.

She had chosen well, it was a lovely evening. Long shadows stretched, finger like across the lawn at the back of the Tea Room. The windows were flung wide open, allowing the white curtains to flutter in the breeze and tangle from time to time with the overgrown honeysuckle.

The garden was small, but in its distant past it had been designed by a skilled hand. A pergola arch ran the full length with untidy rambling roses scrambling over the rustic woodwork.

Harriet smiled lovingly at the group of friends that she had assembled for her all important meeting. "It's so good of you all to come," she said briskly. "I think we are going to have a busy evening. Now, you all know Mr Stevens the pianist, and I expect you remember Val Garratt."

Val laughed, "Mrs Meekham I haven't been away from the village for that many years."

"No, of course you haven't, dear," Harriet replied quickly, "but people do have short memories, and you have changed a great deal since you left us."

"I'm a 'townie' now," and he grinned mischievously. "Would look funny in the London studio with a straw in my teeth trying to teach someone the Tango."

"Yes, I'm sure you would." Harriet was not quite sure whether he was joking or if he was serious. Then a scolding note crept into her voice. "You have changed, though. You look so sophisticated it's positively disgusting. Heaven knows what you must be doing to these poor young things," indicating the girls with a 'broad sweep of her hand, which included an appalled pianist. "Still, I suppose when you have the body of a Greek God it's easy to look sweet in anything."

Val grinned, "Stop flattering, Harriet, I've had enough to be used to it by now, rather bored too, I think."

"Some people thrive on flattery."

"Not me. I can usually see the motive behind it, and sometimes it isn't very nice."

Harriet regarded him sternly, "Do you think I have a motive behind my flattery?"

"I don't know," he frowned, "you're harder to read than most …"

"Now *you* are flattering *me.*"

"… but I think you feel the same as Neil. You want me back in the village."

"So you should be," quietly from the schoolmaster.

"Well, I'm sorry to disappoint you good folk, but I'm stuck in London now, though I don't mind coming up for a visit, or business."

"It would be nice though …" Harriet mused.

Val snorted a laugh his eyes dancing almost as nimbly as his feet did. "Is this a game of 'one up man ship' you're playing, Mrs Meekham?" he questioned playfully. "Are you trying to get an international pianist *and* a well-respected professional ballroom dancer in your village? Do you reckon they would trump the town's Wilmores with all their aristocratic Russian blood?"

"Well …" Harriet shrugged.

"Shame on you," the young man scolded lightly. "I'm afraid you're not getting me, you'll have to make do with Adair and not be greedy."

"Where's Delia?" Melody Harris asked suddenly, "I thought you wanted her to be here."

Val Garrettt grinned, "I promise I haven't done away with her, if that's what you're thinking." Then he added ruefully, "It isn't a case of wanting. I wouldn't touch her if I didn't have to. It's just that I'll need a tall girl if I'm to dance for you, and she fits the bill."

Melody heaved a sigh, wishing that she had been the chosen one. Any girl in the village would have leapt at the chance of dancing with Val Garrettt. "It was a stroke of genius, Harriet persuading her to be your partner," she sighed. "She's got everything the dance needs."

"On the surface I have to agree with you," Val butted in, "but Delia hasn't got the fire the Tango needs. She's a cold fish is that one."

"Don't be cruel," Melody scolded. "You probably have too high a standard. Not everyone is up to your level in dancing."

Val shook his head slowly, his smile gone, "Not everyone is up to my level in height either, and that's the problem. I must say I was sorry that Rosa couldn't come down to partner me, but someone has got to stay and mind the shop. There are a lot of girls in the village that I would gladly teach, but if you want to do an exhibition dance everything has got to be right, and I need a tall girl … like Delia."

"Who isn't here," Harriet sighed.

"Yes, and I wish she would hurry. I want to pace out the space. You don't have much room here for the more flamboyant stuff, and I wouldn't want to knock any of the tables over."

Gloom hovered over the group for a moment, but a click from the door turned all heads in that direction expecting to see the missing dance partner making a late entrance. Instead Beth Riche came quietly into the Tea Room, saying, "I'm sorry I'm late, a swan was caught in a length of abandoned fishing line. We had quite a tussle with it before we could convince it that we meant no harm."

Perhaps it was her plain face, or down to earth manner that set Beth apart from everyone else. Anyone who looked further than the unfashionable but comfortable clothes and neat, tightly drawn back hair would have seen her for the kind, caring soul that she was. Her gentle voice and tender touch would have stolen any blind man's heart. The War had taken the sight of many young men, but none of them lived in the village. Like any other girl she had hoped that one day her knight in shining armour would come and sweep her away, but with each passing year the chances seemed less. So she had guided her life into the paths of charitable works, children, old people, sick dogs, trapped swans all knew her for what she really was, a sweet soul in a plain shell. She was content.

One man had come close to her, but only one. Neil Haily, the boy next door. Four years her senior an inch shorter in height, and by far the better looking of the two, he had watched over her, patient guardian of many years. Unfortunately Neil was now a married man.

"You're dirty," Val remarked, quietly but audibly over the chatter.

Beth followed his intense gaze to her ankles. "I beg your pardon?"

His great mouth curved into a smile, "Mud, you've got a splash on your ankle," then, his eyes flashing and his voice theatrically humble, "Do excuse me looking at your ankles, it's only a professional thing, I do promise you."

Beth laughed, "I'm afraid the swan put up quite a fight, even though it was choking. I thought I'd cleaned myself up."

He sighed, "You should be spending your time looking after a man, not sick animals."

"Don't criticize. Why have you never married? By what I hear you have had enough lady friends?"

Glowering under heavy brows, Val turned away.

Beth smiled softly, saying, "I've got a message from Delia. I'm afraid she has been asked to stay with a friend in Brighton. She's going to be away for some time."

"Now there's a surprise," Val cried.

"You've got an understudy, of course," Beth remarked looking from him to Harriet.

"You mean we did have," Melody answered, "Nicky was going to do it at a pinch, but she seems to be going down with a cold and wasn't feeling at all well."

Harriet caught her breath, "My God, I hope it isn't that dreadful Spanish Flu thing rearing its head again. I did hope that the village was going to be spared."

"I think we've seen the last of that," Beth said softly. "There are fewer and fewer cases reported now."

The owner of the Village Tea Room heaved a sigh. Her Grand Opening was not going to be as grand as she had hoped. "Mr Stevens," she turned to the pianist, "It looks very much as though you will be on your own."

"If I can just have a walk round we might manage," Val said quickly. "As I say, it's such a small space I need to get a feel for it. At a pinch I can persuade Rosa to come down just for the evening."

"Would she mind?" Harriet asked.

"Probably, but she'll come all the same, I'm sure."

Harriet was triumphant, "That's settled then. We will have a dance after all, and when people see you dance, they will want to dance themselves. It will be just like the Tea Room in town."

"But I need someone to walk round with me this evening," Val persisted. "That done, I'll get back to London tomorrow, break the news to Rosa, tell her we only have a postage stamp to dance on, and then bring her down for the opening next ... Saturday is it?"

"Beth can walk round with you," Neil volunteered. "She's about the same height as Delia so you should be comfortable with her."

Beth went white at the suggestion. "No I can't," she cried. "I can't Tango! I don't want to Tango! Ever! By what I've heard it isn't a very nice dance!"

"Rubbish," Val contradicted her immediately. "There's nothing wrong with it. If people would stop throwing their hands in the air every time they hear its name it would soon be popular. Now the Paso Doble ...well, that can be different."

"Never heard of it," Adair commented

Val grinned, "It's come all the way from Paris. It's a sort of Flamenco kind of dance."

"I don't think I would want to dance it then." Melody shook her head sadly. "I've had enough of Spanish things of late."

"You won't have to," Val told her regretfully. He would have loved to master the new dance. "It's too complicated for most people. There are some good steps in it though, they might be injected into other dances. No, I'm afraid the Tango is as far as people will go."

"Well you won't catch me dancing it!" Beth replied sharply.

"Couldn't do it justice in this small space," the expert told her. "No, just a quick spin round with a Waltz should be good enough. It will give me some ideas to take back to London."

"Come on Beth," Adair seated himself at the little piano that had been tucked away in a corner. He tried a few notes and frowned. "This won't do if I'm to play, where did you get it, Mrs Meekham?"

"It was in the cellar at the house," Harriet said with a sigh, feeling that things were rapidly getting too complicated for her to deal with. "Don't say you want to pull out of the opening. If you do, I shall have to borrow Mrs Jenkins gramophone, and someone will have to sit by it winding the handle and putting on the records."

Adair smiled, "Don't worry, I'll get you another one, and I promise it won't come out of a cellar. What music do you want, Val?"

"Just a Waltz, nothing fancy," Val rose to his feet, bowed, and held out his hand in invitation. "Miss Riche, will you do me the honour … and I promise not to Tango or Paso a single step, but I might tread on your feet for a bit."

"Don't be silly, Val," Beth scolded, taking his hand and letting him lead her into the tiny dancing space.

The couple did a turn round the floor to the tune of the 'out of tune' piano.

"Don't hunch your shoulders," Val said calmly. "You've no need to lose height. I am quite tall enough to manage you. You have a beautiful neck, just like your swan. *Ow! Blast!*"

"I'm sorry," In trying to concentrate on her shoulders Beth had completely forgotten what her feet were doing.

"We aren't marching, we are Waltzing, smaller steps if you don't mind."

With an indignant cry Beth pushed from him. "I'm doing my best," she said sharply, "If I'm not up to your standards, then it's too bad. I didn't ask to dance with you."

"Yes, and I can see why. Come on, let's try again."

Reluctantly Beth allowed him to once more take hold of her.

"If you've finished squabbling I'll continue," Adair commented dryly and did so all the same.

"Well," Val sighed at last, "there isn't going to be much room to display, but I think we can manage something. I supposed the customers will just want to hold close and shuffle. Good luck to them too, I say. There's nothing like a … a …" His eyes fixed on his partner's face. "You've gone quite pink, Beth," he remarked with twinkling eyes.

"This," Beth replied, once more pushing from him and taking to her chair, "is something I never, ever, want anyone to remind me of."

Chapter 2

The evening wore on, suggestions were made ideas talked over, a program of entertainment decided on.

"I'm tired," Melanie said at last, stifling a yawn, "I didn't sleep well last night. I was dreaming of Ralph."

"He'll be back one day, just you wait and see." Neil touched her hand sympathetically. He had perfect faith in the absent soldier's homing instinct, but even he had to admit to some concern as to why he was taking so long to leave the hospital.

"Have you not tried to visit him?" Harriet asked, knowing that she would have been battering the ward doors down if her husband was incarcerated for any length of time.

"I did ask," Melony swallowed. She had been about to marry Ralph Witham when war broke out and he had gone away. She had not seen him for nearly six years, but her love for him had not diminished. "They told me that he had refused to see anyone and they were respecting his wishes."

"I suppose that's understandable," Harriet sighed. "They say he was badly wounded."

"Depends on how much of a man he was to begin with," Sam Freeman snorted. He had lost a leg in the war, but he was still as much a man as any there. As soon as he was out of hospital he had come home to the town and his aging mother. Hester Freeman had never forgiven her son for being a conscientious objector, even though he had been taken on as a stretcher bearer and wounded twice while carrying out his duty. To her he had not won his medal, but simply been given it 'because that was what they did.'

Sam had been hurt by her sharp words, hurt even more when she told him that she did not want him in her house. He had been hoping to marry Winnie Bransome and start life at home while they saved enough money for a place of their own. That was the first of his plans to go wrong. The second was that there was no work for him in town, even more reason for his mother to want her useless son out of her house.

Then Winnie had given him a piece of her mind. In a month they were married and renting a run-down flat on the outskirts of town. Harriet Meekham's offer of the cottage and position of manager for her Tea Room had been a God sent blessing for them both.

"Have you written to him?" Beth asked.

"Twice," was the unhappy reply. "Matron wrote a lovely note, full of sympathy, she said he tore my letters up and told them any more were to be returned unopened."

"Did he indeed," quietly from Neil, and even more quietly, "we must see about that."

Evening had become night and suddenly with Melody's yawn everyone began to feel tired. Once more Harriet thanked Beth for stepping into the breach and everyone left, content that the Grand Opening was going to be a success.

Adair and the Freemans returned to their cottages further along the lane. Already Mrs Freeman was planning the catering for the opening. As soon as he was in his own living room Adair began to sort out the problem of the piano. Neil insisted on escorting Melody across the common to her house near the church and Val paired off with Beth, who wished he would let her walk home on her own because his presence was making her feel nervous.

They strolled down the street in silence, his hands linked loosely behind his back, hers swinging by her sides. The soft perfumes of the summer night wafted to them from each of the neatly kept front gardens.

"You're not very good at dancing, are you," he said at last as they neared the village green and the memorial cross.

Beth shrugged sadly, "I don't get the practice. I haven't been to a dance for a long time. I gave up. I never get invited onto the floor. I'm too tall and …"

"So you hunch your shoulders."

"Yes, I suppose I do."

There was another short pause, while the leather soles of his finely crafted shoes snapped impatiently on the pavement. "It's nice to be alone for a while," he said at last, glancing up at the village cross.

"It's nice to be out on such an evening," Beth replied. "Just look at those stars."

He stopped, and shook his head. For a moment he gazed at the towering grey monument, and then he said, with a sigh, "What I couldn't say in front of the others was, I don't like Delia. I'm glad she didn't come and I had a chance to dance with you." In all the time he had been away Beth had not changed. She was still a solemn, solitary person. Then he said suddenly, "Beth, if you're so concerned about dancing, why did you do it back there?"

"You needed a partner."

"So you allowed yourself to be sacrificed on the altar of the dance floor."

"Something like that."

He sank onto the soft turf at the foot of the cross, and leaned on the bottom step, "I've hardly ever had a chance to talk to you since I went to London. Sit down let's enjoy a moment away from them all."

"All right, but not for long." She sat on the bottom step, near to his hand.

"Look," he said in a very low voice, "I suppose it's because of my profession, but I believe everyone should have a chance to dance at least once in their lifetime. When Rosa and I have finished our business at the Grand Opening, I'd be glad to partner you."

She smiled down into his serious upturned face, "That seems like a very good offer, but …"

He picked a daisy out of the grass and twirled it in his fingers, "You were embarrassed back there. You don't want to repeat the performance."

"Of course not. There was nothing ..."

"Don't deny it, I was holding you, remember, I could feel you trembling."

Beth could do no other than remember that he had been holding her. One hand as large as her own had been holding hers while the other had rested on her waist drawing her to him. It was no wonder that a girl who had never been held close to a man before had started trembling. "I meant it when I said I didn't want to be reminded of the incident," she replied. But was that true? She knew without a doubt that tonight she would go home her head as giddy as a sixteen year old after her first ball and she would remember time and again the moment when Val Garrett, the darling of London society had held her in his arms. Val Garrett who partnered the beautiful dark haired Rosa and was applauded where ever he went.

Suddenly he sprang to his feet and grabbing her hand hauled her up to stand beside him. "Dammit, Beth," he said sharply. "You will dance with me at the opening. When Rosa and I have finished I will come looking for you, and if you have run away and locked yourself in your house I shall send Neil after you. He won't let you hide." Then while she was still dazed by his words and actions, he slapped his arm about her. "Don't hunch and small steps," he ordered. "No one's watching, well the stars are but they won't tell, so if you tread on my feet a few times it doesn't matter. Dance with me, Beth, and we will surprise them all on the great day!"

"I'm so tall," she murmured.

"Granny says, 'Pines are nearer heaven than birches', try to remember that."

"I'll try."

"Good, now, relax for heaven's sake or we won't get anywhere. I'm going to give you a lesson you won't forget easily."

"Like you give your dancing partners."

He laughed noiselessly, his great form shaking, "People do talk. I seldom lay a finger on those girls off the dance floor. I don't know why they say all those things about us."

"You are a bit of a gigolo, though. Go on, admit it. You've had so many partners before Rosa. Why? What are you looking for?"

He sighed, "Perfection, I suppose. They all look so beautiful at first. I see them, dance with them, and finish with them. They are either too short or too heavy, or something ... Sometimes I can't get rid of them quick enough. Of course, the one woman I could dance with for the rest of my life is pining for someone else."

"Who's that?"

"Melody Harris. Beautiful in name and face."

"And there is no one else?"

He considered the point for a moment, "If your Neil ..."

"He isn't my Neil."

"Well he dammed well should have been ... If your Neil hadn't snapped up little Lindy, I might have had a go at her. I couldn't dance with her, but I could have loved her."

Beth laughed and stood still causing him to crash into her and give her a stern look. "Val, you're being silly. You are right, though, they are both beautiful as well as talented."

"Beauty, I love it." He smiled down at her. She had relaxed completely while they talked and his instinct told him that if she would only allow herself to, she would make a reasonable dancer. "But beauty doesn't have to be in a woman's face, Beth," he said suddenly. It can be in her soul as well. That is a very rare beauty and one Delia will never know." He casually tapped at her toe and was delighted when she began to move again.

"You have a pretty girl with a true heart in Rosa," she told him. "People are saying that you must be falling in love with her, or you wouldn't have kept her as a partner for so long."

"People don't know I wanted to ditch her a few months back."

"Really, Val! Think of the convenience. When you were away you would only need one hotel room."

"Some folk think we have that in any case."

"Yes, I know. I really think you should do something about it before the gossip goes too far."

"Doesn't it matter if I'm not in love with the girl?"

"But they talk so."

He smiled and shook his head, "I'm a dancer, Beth," he said ruefully. "If it had been ballet they would have called me other, nastier names. There's nothing between me and Rosa and she cares as little about gossip as I do. Our consciences are clear. Mind you," his eyes sparkled in the moonlight, "I'm not saying that given the right girl and the right place I couldn't live up to all they say, but it hasn't happened, yet."

"It's hard to believe."

"It's Gran," he said at last, "When I get hold of some of those girls I do go a bit light headed, I am only human after all. Then I think of all she has taught me. Oh, Granny Drummond is a great one for seeing through a person. As soon as I start to see them through her eyes all the glitter goes with the ball dress. I usually see an ugly little soul reaching out for the chance of a good life, with glamour and excitement, and me thrown in for good measure. Once it gets to that pitch, I make the break."

"I wish I could meet your grandmother."

His eyes flashed, "I wish you could, but I'd hate to be there. You'd be having me over before I knew where I was."

They had stopped dancing once more. Hardly realising what he was doing he cupped her face in his great hands and was just bending his head to kiss her when a polite cough broke the enchantment and a voice over to their right said, "Don't you think you had better both go home?" Neil had returned from seeing Melody across the common.

Beth leapt back, her cheeks colouring with embarrassment. Val's eyes were daggers as he glared at the other man. Suddenly he wanted to knock him down.

Neil nodded and half smiled. Then he held out his hand. "Come Beth, I'll see you to your door and Val can return to his lodgings."

Beth left her partner without a word, glancing back at him with wide, startled eyes.

"Thanks' for the chat," he said breathlessly. "Don't ever be afraid of dancing again. You'll find there's nothing to it, really. All you have to do is relax."

She smiled, and let Neil take her hand, "I'll try," she replied. She had always sworn that if a man tried to kiss her uninvited she would scratch his eyes out. Now she had simply given in, and enjoyed it rather. She smiled, her finger tips to her lips. This was different though. It had been no more than a friendly gesture. Val was like that.

"Home is in this direction, if you remember," Neil said quietly at her side.

She jumped and turned to him, her face flushed, her eyes shining. In that moment of awakening she could never have guessed how different she looked. "I'm sorry I was ... I mean ..." she stopped to collect her thoughts, "Val has been helping me to dance."

"Oh, has he?"

"Well, perhaps he was being a little silly as well."

"Perhaps." But the other man's actions had not looked in the least silly to Neil as he had come down the street to join them.

Chapter 3

"Beth? Beth, where have you taken yourself off to? If you don't come out at once I'll send for Neil."

Saturday evening had come. The Village Tea Room was officially open and ready for business.

It had been a splendid opening. Adair had played Chopin and at Harriet's special request the Liszt Consolation number 3. Then Val and Rosa had danced to the music of Strauss. They had composed a dazzling program, beautiful and swirling for such a small space. Everyone agreed that they were a perfect couple, he so handsome in his evening wear and she exquisite in gold and lace.

Now Rosa was talking to Sandy Witham and Val had come hunting for Beth. For a moment he had thought that he was going to have to carry out his threat and send the schoolteacher to find her. Then he caught a glimpse of her in the overgrown garden.

"Oh heaven help us!" he cried. "What are you doing down there?"

Beth came out of her hiding place behind the bushes. She had been standing there for the biggest part of the evening, well out of sight but able to watch what was happening through the open door.

"I'm sorry," she murmured, "I didn't want to be in the way." It was no excuse and she knew it, but suddenly she could not think of anything better to say.

"Come on, my dance, I believe," he said, grabbing her hand to haul her unwillingly into the Tea Room and onto the dancing space. "Don't worry, I won't let you make a fool of yourself."

Several couples were already on their feet. Chet and Sara were off in a corner, holding very close and 'shuffling.' Dancing was unimportant to them. What mattered was the chance to get their hands on each other. Rosa was trying to explain an intricate step to Sandy Witham who was out to impress his current sweetheart. She was a patient teacher. He was not a very apt pupil.

"Small steps and …" Val began.

"I know, don't hunch!" Beth cut in rather more sharply than she had intended.

"Swan neck, remember." He nodded, sensing her nervousness. "Get it right and you never know, someone might want to take a turn round the floor with you. That can lead to all sorts of things."

Unwillingly Beth shuffled her feet to the tune of the music unaware that they had remembered the lesson at the village cross, even though her head seemed to have forgotten it. Val did not criticize this time, but as more couples joined them in the small space he held his partner closer and smiled into her hair, satisfied that she had straightened her shoulders at last.

They paused for a moment as Sam Freeman took Adair's place at the piano. His wife had been itching to dance and the pianist soon had her as his partner. Val gave Beth's toe a tap and they began moving again. How comfortable she felt in his arms. Of all the girls he had danced with she was the perfect height. Given the chance on a decent floor he could have taught her more steps. They could have amazed and delighted an audience together. Then he glanced at Rosa, beautiful Rosa who was smiling so sweetly at him. No, that was the face the public wanted to see as his partner, not this plain homely face that was resting on his shoulder lost in the magic of the music. This face was the one to be kept in some safe sacred spot away from public glare, worshiped and adored as a wife and mother should be. If only that moment could last for ever. If only the music would never end.

But end it did. The perfect evening was almost over and it was time to go home. Beth would return to her hum-drum life in the village, Val to the glamour and enchantment of London and later the Continent.

"Good girl," he murmured as the spell was finally broken and she pushed self-consciously away from him, her cheeks colouring. "You did well."

She smiled, gaining some reassurance from his words, and the warm squeeze of his hand. "Did I?" she asked. "Are you sure I didn't hunch again?"

"It was..." he paused, the tight feeling in his throat making it difficult to speak, "it was perfect," he murmured.

"Silly boy."

Suddenly they embraced, "I knew you could do it," he murmured over the top of her head.

Beth laughed softly. It was her moment of triumph. Above all people he knew what that was like. "And I didn't make a fool of myself?"

"My dear, you can believe me, you were perfect." He was still dazed, the closer he held her the more his body throbbed. It was a new experience for Val Garratt. His dancing partners knew only too well that his flashing eyes and dark looks were only a front put on for the public. Under it all he was a cold fish in a steamy Latin American shell.

"Oh, come now I can't have been that," perhaps she sensed the change, and strained back from him.

"You were beautiful, tonight."

"Don't flatter, I don't need it."

He released her slightly, and took both of her hands in his, "I wasn't flattering. The eyes are the portals to the soul. Tonight as we danced, I looked into your eyes and what I saw was beautiful."

Beth broke away from him, her heart giving a sudden hard beat before seeming to stand completely still. "I think that's enough, Val," she scolded softly. Then, pulling herself together, she turned and slipped once more through the door and out into the overgrown garden. It was cool and refreshing there. Somewhere under the tangle of vegetation a hopeful bloom was filling the night air with perfume. Bending, she brushed back the overgrowing leaves and discovered a valiant clump of Mrs Sinkins Pinks, named after Catherine Sinkins who had died only a few years before. The liberated blooms seemed to fill the garden with their fragrance and she drew a long deep breath of the heady air. Everyone should be allowed to share this pleasure and she decided that as soon as she could get Harriet to herself, she would tackle her on having the garden tidied.

Val stood in the doorway watching as she picked one small blossom and bent her head to inhale its scent. There was such tenderness and strength in the tall gangly form that he almost cried with joy watching her.

Melody passed him on the way to the buffet tables and paused, "Val, dear, are you all right?" she questioned softly, following his gaze. There was no answer, and with a sweet smile she went away.

He scarcely knew that she had been there, for he was watching Beth, watching her as he had never watched a woman before.

She did not stay long. A sudden loneliness came over her. She too had experienced new emotions that night, and longed for the company of her old ladies, or even a swan. There was nothing like a tussle with an irate swan to make one forget a problem.

The whole night was ahead of her. She felt sure that she would not sleep, and if she did the face of Val Garrett would haunt her dreams. What had happened to them back there? Was he going to start collecting village girls as well as dancing partners? Was she to be the first of a new line?

Suddenly she wanted go home, back to her sanctuary among the lilac trees. There she would think about the man who had treated her differently to any other man before.

A hand shot out and took hold of her arm as she entered the Tea Room. Val had been waiting by the door for her to return. His face was white, but the fire had gone from his eyes. Lost in her thoughts she had not noticed anyone there and the movement made her start. She looked up at him, torn between the impulse to run, and an urge to throw her arms about him and carry on where they had left off.

"May I walk you home?" he asked huskily.

She nodded mutely. She was on strange ground, and it frightened her, "You'll miss the end of the party if you come back now," she said.

"I'm not missing anything if I am walking my partner home."

"Your partner?" She laughed, "I'm no more your partner than any of the other village girls. You were very much in demand, you know"

"Was I? I really don't remember them."

Now she began to feel more at ease, "Oh really, Val, how silly you've become."

"Don't laugh, I'm serious."

"Sorry, dear, but it didn't sound like you."

"You were perfect. I saw Rosa smile when we were together. She knows. I'll wager you'll get several proposals of marriage after tonight."

"You make me sound dreadful."

"You danced well tonight. That is far from dreadful."

"What about the other girls, Val? Did none of them dance well?"

He shook his head, "I'm not interested in little girls."

"Aren't you?" Her eyes sparkled like stars as he accompanied her down the lane leading to the village. Then as he looked cross, "I'm sorry. Have you got an ideal, though? Most of your partners are dark, you admire Lindy she is dark also."

He shrugged his broad shoulders, "Perhaps they are all dark, but the outside appearance means nothing to me. It's what a woman is like inside that counts," then glancing at her from the corner of his eye, "And you, what about your ideal man?"

Beth answered quickly and without hesitation, "I haven't got one."

"Any man will be good enough?"

"Not any man, he must be ..." she sighed, "I suppose I'd know if ever I met him."

Val nodded, "Believe me, you would know, sooner or later."

They had reached her door, and he took her key to open it, "I'll not come in, don't ask. I want to go for a long walk and think about my ideal woman, good night, Beth."

"Good night, Val," she took her key back from his warm hand, finding it bewilderingly difficult to look into his face, "Thank you for helping me. I do appreciate it," then with a parting smile, "Don't stay out too late or you might catch a chill, and it will spoil your performance on the Continent."

She went into the house and slowly mounted the stairs. From her bedroom window she watched his tall well-built figure, beautiful in black evening wear, as he began his solitary walk in the night. He was an artist, an artist to his fingertips. Some of the emotion that went into his beloved Latin American dancing had overflowed into real life. That was it. It had been a dramatic performance for a dramatic occasion. On Monday when he danced with Rosa again he would forget all about her.

Of course his partner was the answer to all the problems. He must be made to see that.

He would have to marry Rosa Hinds. Once that was done, he might really settle down, and once settled his partners in their pretty dresses would fade away, and he would think of her. That done, his skills combined with his smouldering good looks, would soon get them to the top.

She undressed slowly and got into bed, her thoughts on Val Garrett all the while. Her body, more tired than she guessed, took over from her weary mind, and she sank into a deep sleep.

Out in the moonlight, Val Garrett stuck his great hands deep into his pockets and stared up at the Celtic cross. Suddenly to him it was the symbol of all the emotions that were only now awakening in him. He thought of the years he had known her. The way she had encouraged him when he was a shop assistant in the little shop on the outskirts of the village. No one else had faith in him. They called him names when he said that he wanted to make a career of dancing. If they had taken the trouble to drop in at the dancing school and watch him at practice, they would have changed their minds. Only Melody and Beth ever came. Beth just a couple of times to be kind, because dancing meant so little to her, and Melody quite often because he was a friend of Ralph Witham and she had almost adopted him.

A few eyebrows had been raised when he started entering competitions. No one had thought that he was good enough. Some came down on his side when he began carrying off the first prizes. Then there was the big problem with his partners. None of the girls had been to his liking until Rosa. They both knew from the moment they took their first steps together that theirs could be a worthwhile partnership. For hours they practiced together, his shirt stuck to his back with sweat, and Rosa trying to smile as she limped round with a sore ankle, where his great feet had taken the wrong turn.

He thought of the day when they had decided to turn professional. The shop keeper, dear old soul, had shook his hand and wished him luck. Beth had wished him luck too. She knew the couples ambition, to gain all the experience they could, and then open their own dancing school.

Before, when he danced, his partner had meant little to him. It was just another part of his job, like a pair of handmade shoes. Now it would never be the same, because he would think of Beth, and all that he could be holding in his arms.

Chapter 4

A steady stream of pebbles tapping her window, roused Beth from her sleep and a voice which she knew only too well, called to her urgently from below.

She stumbled out of bed. Flinging on her dressing gown she drew aside the curtain and leaned out of the window. "Val," she hissed, "it's the middle of the night. What do you want?"

"I want to talk to you," he replied softly.

"You can't it's too late."

"I want to talk about getting married."

"Have you had too much to drink?" and she pulled her dressing gown tighter about her throat.

"You know I haven't. Do be a good girl and come down. It's awfully difficult shouting quietly. I can't raise my voice or I'll have Gregory taking my name and address for disturbing the peace. If he doesn't nab me, your watchdog will," he nodded in the direction of Neil Haily's house. "Why do you live among such formidable neighbours? Be an angel and let me in."

"But I'm not dressed."

His eyes sparkled roguishly in the moonlight, "All the better."

She sighed, "I'll come down for a few minutes, but you must give me time to put some clothes on. In your present mood you're not setting a foot in the house while I'm like this."

Her head disappeared from the window, and she shut it firmly. He whistled an air from 'Pinafore', and did a quick shanty, stopping to look round and grin as she opened the door.

"Now, Val," she said briskly, "come in and get it off your chest."

He entered the house, and sat on the old fashioned chintzy covered sofa.

"Do you want me to make a cup of tea?"

"If you want one," he could put it off that long.

"I think I will, it might steady you down," and then she added in a scolding tone, "Val, you do look disturbed."

"I feel it too. Stop criticising, woman, and make the tea. I want a serious talk with you."

She smiled over the tea pot as she warmed it and wondered what had made him call at such a late hour. Quite unprepared for what was to come, she returned to him and poured the tea.

He sipped it thoughtfully, then set down the bone china cup, and stared at his hands.

"Well, Val," she prompted, "You were so full of it, now you have nothing to say."

"It's because I don't know how to begin," he replied quietly, "There is so much I have to tell you. Beth, I'm going to need every ounce of patience you've got before this night's out." He ran his fingers through his dark hair, "How can I put it into words? I've never felt much for anyone, well, there is one I worship above all others, but as she is seventy five years old," she knew by this that he meant his grandmother, "you need have no fear of competition from her. You know I admire Melody, and Linda, but there is a feeling growing more every minute. It's growing so frighteningly fast that I'm not quite sure what to do with it. That's why I want your help. You are so very much involved."

"Drink your tea, Val, before it gets cold," she was not being hard on him, and did not want to put him off, but the simple act of tea drinking might give him a moment in which to collect his thoughts.

Automatically he did as he was told, "At last I've found a woman to love," he went on. "I don't think I knew what the word meant until tonight. Then I realised what real love is. Oh, Beth, I'll never make you understand."

She could not speak. It suddenly seemed as though he belonged there in her front room, drinking her tea. If only it could be like that for ever. The feeling of emptiness the house had was gone, two people were there, telling secrets that only the four walls should hear. Even as she thought it, he looked into her eyes, his own flashing as they had at the dance, and said the last thing she ever expected to hear.

"Beth, I want you for my wife."

She felt a wave of panic sweep over her. Surely he had come to talk about Rosa. Her cheeks were burning, she was blushing, a fact that embarrassed her even more. "Are you asking me to marry you?"

"In a clumsy way … yes."

She stared at him across the room, "I thought we were discussing Rosa."

"I came to ask *you.*" His voice was calm, his decision had been made. "I didn't want to talk about Rosa, she has a brilliant pair of feet, and a faultless sense of timing, I could wish no more in a dancing partner, but for the partner in life I want other things."

Beth stood up and for want of something to do, fiddled aimlessly with the teapot. He had taken her utterly by surprise. "Val, I had no idea." She twisted her hands together, and looked down into his dark brooding features, "I can't give you an answer directly. I didn't think that you held me any closer than a friend."

"I could hold you much closer than I have held any friend."

"But I thought you wanted to talk about Rosa," she persisted, not letting him interrupt her for long, "If I had thought for one moment that it was otherwise, I would not have let you into the house at this time of night."

"You're safe."

She ignored him, "Everyone expects you to marry your partner. There is the fact that you are always going away together."

"Let them think what they will." There was a note of defiance in his voice, and his bright eyes flashed as he watched her, adoring her frank honest face more with every passing minute. "You know the truth of the matter now."

"I must have time to think."

He tapped the seat beside him, "Come and sit down, we'll talk it over."

"No," Beth stayed firmly on the other side of the room, "You'll not talk me into it, Val, I hold marriage as sacred, not entered into lightly, or carelessly broken. I have seen what scatter brained marriages can do. That is not for me. I thought the time had come when no man would ask me to marry him. It is a shock to know that it could be otherwise."

Val did not answer. If he had at that minute, he would have leapt up grabbing her shoulders and shaking her till her teeth rattled, probably telling her meanwhile to stop acting like a child and grow up. Instead he sat silently, studying the pattern on the carpet.

When he could trust himself, he said, "But don't you feel anything between us? Is it all on my side?"

"I feel that we must be cautious. I'll give you my answer as soon as I can."

He rose to her feet and taking up her hands looked steadily into her clear grey eyes, "You haven't got long," he said, "I return to London tomorrow, and then we leave for the Continent. I cannot dance with a heart the weight of lead, wondering what your answer will be."

Beth struggled with her emotions, it would have been so nice to throw her arms round his neck and kiss him as she had never expected to kiss a man. But she was nearly thirty. Was she just jumping at what might be the only chance of marriage that she would get? She pushed him towards the door. "Tomorrow afternoon by the weir," will that be good enough?"

He nodded, "I can wait that long, if you promise to give me your answer, but after that I must make a dash for London."

She opened the door and let him out, "I promise," she said.

He stood in the doorway for a moment, took her shoulders in his great hands, and kissed her lightly on the lips, then with a wistful smile he turned and walked away.

The sound of his footsteps echoed on the path outside. In no time at all he was gone, and she went back to the front room, to sit in her chair and stare unbelievingly at the corner of the sofa where he had sat not five minutes before. Once again the house was empty. She could feel it even more acutely now, and wished that she had someone, even a sick animal in her care, that she could turn to.

She shook herself up, and standing, went to the small mahogany table where he had set his cup. The room was spinning as she went to pick it up, and she fell sobbing into his place, her hand knocking over the frail china vessel, and sending it crashing to the floor, where it lay cracked into three parts on the carpet. She remembered how calm he had been, if he felt then what she was suffering now, the effort must have been tremendous.

She did not know that she stopped crying, or that she fell asleep, but suddenly there was a pain in her arm, which was twisted under her, and she looked at the clock to find that almost an hour had passed.

She stood up stiffly, glanced at the broken cup, and stooped to pick it up. The set had a place on the dresser, although she would not be able to use it again, she must mend the broken one, and put it back where it belonged. That must be for tomorrow through, tonight she must go back to bed and try to get another hour's sleep.

Slowly she mounted the stairs, his words ringing over and over in her ears until she felt that she would scream. She had no idea how to answer him, it seemed such a short time.

Val stopped by the village cross, he had made a hash of it, but he couldn't understand how. He had thought that she must feel the same as he did. Was it just kindness that made her as she was towards him? If so, then she was more kind to him than she was to anyone else, and that didn't sound at all like Beth.

"Dear God," he prayed, "I want her for my wife."

There was no answer. Perhaps the trees rustled their shadowy branches, but that was all.

He went to the foot of the cross, and laid his hand on it, "I'd make any sacrifice to win her," he went on, thinking of his ornate dancing trophies and realising that compared to Beth they were of little worth. "She's more precious to me than anything I own," but there was only emptiness, and he sighed, and went home.

Chapter 5

The next afternoon, her heart full of fears, Beth made her way across the cornfield in the direction of the river. It was such a beautiful spot. On one side was the lock, where the jaunty little boats with their colourful awnings and pennants took their loads of day trippers up and down past the old castle. On the other side the weir gushed and roared, flashing white foam along the bank.

Val was there leaning on the style, waiting patiently. He looked up in her direction and knew instinctively by the reluctance of her step what her answer would be. The next few minutes were going to be difficult for both of them.

He came to meet her, his eyes burning with fire. "I believe we have something to discuss," he said, holding out his hand.

She let him lead her along the stony path towards the spot where he had been leaning. There he helped her sit on a fence, while he leaned, one foot up on the style beside her.It was a classic scene, the fields and the river, Val so young, so broodingly handsome. To

Beth only one thing spoiled the beauty of it all, and that was herself.

"Have you made up your mind?" he asked, dreading the answer.

She nodded. "Yes," she replied.

"What have you decided?"

She looked at him, his eyes on a herd of cows just visible through the trees on the other side of the river, "I'm sorry, Val, I can not marry you."

There was silence. The colour drained slowly from his face, and in a moment of panic she almost gave in. Then reason took hold once more. There could never be a place for a plain awkward girl like Beth Riche in a scene with Val Garrett. She was being kind to them both in turning him down.

"May I know your reason?"

"It's simply that I don't think I'm the right person for you."

"I asked you. Do you doubt my judgement?"

"Of course not," she twisted her big hands together. It had been bad enough refusing the first time, was he going to make her repeat it, "You have my answer ... It's for your good as well as mine."

"Beth ..." he turned to her, his face set and mask like.

"Yes?" she waited, but he could not speak. She said, "You fell in love with me when we danced, the same as you fall in love with so many girls. But one day the music would stop and we would not dance any more."

"I see," he sighed and straightened up, "I'm glad you've told me. It would have been the devil to go away and then come back to this. I'll not bother you again. Good bye, Elizabeth."

She watched bewildered as he walked away. He had taken it, just like that. Did he think so little of her that he was letting her off the hook so easily? Deep in her heart she knew that she had done the right thing. One day on the dance floor he would look at Rosa, and realize that she was the perfect partner, both for dance and life.

With all her heart she wished him luck, and knew that her life would be empty now. In that brief spell he had awakened in her a yearning that no one else could ease. She slid sadly from the fence, and cut across the corn field, the nearest way to her home. It would hurt to see Val married to someone else, but it was better for him to have Rosa as a wife. Heavy of heart she turned into the back street, where in its nest of lilac trees her little cottage awaited her.

From that day there were often reports of Val's progress in the local newspaper, and Beth followed them with interest. They had been welcomed stiffly when they first went abroad, but after a while, Val's charm and Rosa's beauty won their audiences over. Now they went from strength to strength, sure of a welcome on any dance floor. Paris had been particularly kind and she wondered if they had learned the complicated new Paso, what ever it was called, while they were there.

During the War she had often dropped in to read the newspaper for several of the local old folk who with failing eyesight were unable to read it themselves. The grandmothers had yearned for news of sons and grandsons away fighting. The grandfathers had been more interested in the progress made, though at times that was precious little.

Now she still read the news to a few. Many of them remembered Val as a scruffy little urchin scampering about the village, usually in the company of Ralph and Neil, though even then Neil had done very little by way of 'scampering.' All of them wanted to know what their 'local boy' was doing abroad.

As she read the reports, all of the feelings she had tried so hard to smother came stealing back. When the pair returned to home soil there had been a reporter from a national newspaper waiting to greet them. It was sure evidence that they were beginning to make a name for themselves. Few people in England had seen them dance so well. In Europe their talent had bloomed. They moved as one, Rosa knew every step that he would take. Theirs was a skill which in time was guaranteed to make the headlines in all the newspapers. Audiences stood to applaud night after night, and hopeful couples for dancing competitions knew their chances were slim if this remarkable pair took part.

Miss Vida and Miss Gertrude, two elderly unmarried sisters both adored Val.

Miss Vida expressed a wish that he would return to the village. Her sister would have none of it.

"They're all like that, they get a bit of money and they don't want to live in a quiet little place like this," she commented scornfully. "Got to have the bright lights of the city all the time."

"He's not married to her yet, is he," Miss Vida remarked.

Vicious old biddies, Beth thought, resenting them for him in his absence.

"Probably don't need to be," her sister replied. "You can't tell me those separate hotel rooms are always occupied."

"Yes," Miss Vida sighed, "they share the same house in London too."

That was no longer true. In the beginning the pair had invested every penny they had in a large property in one of the better London suburbs. The ground floor had been devoted to a dance studio while Val and Rosa lived, 'above the shop,' as he called it. It was only natural that those who did not know the couple should come to the wrong conclusions.

Beth turned her attention to the current edition of the local news. The pair had just won a dancing competition, the name of which meant nothing to her. It was a victory all the same, and that was important.

In the interview that followed the presentation, the reporter had remarked on the success of their summer tour of the Continent.

"Yes, we are going back again next year," Val had replied.

Beth choked as she read the words. He would be out of the country more than in it, if he kept this up. Adair Stevens was known internationally as a concert pianist, but he spent most of his time on British soil.

In the photograph which accompanied the article Val looked virtually the same. His eyes were as bright, the only difference was a hard little line creeping into the corner of his mouth. He seemed to be changing with success.

Then the reporter asked what everyone wanted to know. Were there any plans for the couple to marry? Val replied quickly that they had no plans concerning marriage, the present arrangement being quite adequate.

Miss Vida and Miss Gertrude enjoyed that little gem of information.

"It's sinful!" Miss Gertrude exclaimed, adding hurriedly, "Read on, girl."

Then came news which Beth had not previously heard.

Val had invested in a second house, close to their first. It was not for a special retreat when they did marry, he assured the reporter, but for the one person he held above all others, his grandmother.

Trying not to be surprised, the reporter concluded that this only went to prove what a wonderful couple these young people were.

Beth went home, her heart throbbing. She paused on her doorstep. Then taking her courage in both hands went to the house next door and rapped hard on the knocker.

Linda came, pretty little dark haired Linda, who Val admired. "Beth," she cried, "what is it? Are you feeling lonely?"

"I want to talk to Neil," she replied.

Linda's dark eyebrows shot up. "Then you had better come in."

They went into the Haily's front room. Neil snapped the book he was reading shut and leapt up to greet his visitor. "We haven't seen you for some time, Beth," he said, offering her a chair. "What's the matter? Feeling lonely?"

"I wanted a father confessor," she replied. "You know I always come to you."

Neil looked up quickly, "Tea, Linda," he said, and as his wife left the room, "Now, tell me all about it, Beth."

She sank into an antique chair near the fireplace, and put her long hand over her eyes, "Oh, Neil, I think I've made such a terrible blunder."

Neil sat in silence, Linda brought the tea, and left immediately, explaining that she was going to do some ironing.

Beth sipped the tea before going on, "Neil, I gave something up because I believed deep down that it was wrong for me to have it. After several months, I'm still feeling the loss and I don't know what to do."

His cup chinked as he placed it in the saucer, "Can you tell me the details?"

"Val asked me to marry him. I turned him down." She looked at him, too small and gentle with his mild blue eyes and flaxen hair to be the rock that so many people saw him as. "I can't go on living like this. I want to get away from here, but I don't know where to go."

"You want to leave the village for ever?"

"No, I want a holiday, to go away and think of things. The village is part of me, but at the minute it is the sick part, and either it must be treated or I'm sure I'll die."

"Don't be so melodramatic. I'd expect a speech like that from Delia, not from you." He thought for a moment, then drawing his light brows down hard together, said, "I think you should go abroad for a year. See Belgium, see what they have suffered due to the war. I am sure you would soon realise your problems are small in comparison."

"I'm sure I would," Beth sighed, "but it would just be more devastation. I need somewhere quiet away from the village where I can rest, and relax … and think."

"I see." He was silent for a moment, then he said, "Adair Stevens goes to a guest house called Whitesands. It's on the coast and has beautiful views of the sea, I believe.

Then again, if you want real solitude, you could talk to Joel Meekham."

"Joel?"

"He has a friend in the Welsh valleys. A good man with a good wife, I believed, and if all Joel says is true, the local priest is a fine man, too."

Beth was immediately interested. "That sounds ideal. You are a darling." She smiled for the first time for days. "I'll go and talk to Harriet and Joel. While I'm there I'll have a word with them about the garden at the back of the Tea Room. Harriet really should do something about it."

True to her word Beth was soon hammering on the door at Gannilea.

"Oh, my dear," Harriet exclaimed on hearing the news, "Evans farm is just the place to go if you want to forget something! It must rank only second in the world to the Foreign Legion in being remote!"

"It sounds ideal," Beth agreed. She had not given Harriet the full details, only Neil and Linda had those because she knew that secrets were safe with them. All she had said was that she had a problem on her mind and wanted to go out of the village to think about it.

Joel Meekham came into the house, smiling when he saw Beth and greeting her warmly. "My dear girl, I should think Evans will be delighted to have you for a while," he said, on hearing their plans. "If you want solitude, then that's the place to go. I can vouch for that. The nearest village is a couple of miles away and the town ... well, I doubt if you would want to walk the distance."

Beth nodded, "Solitude is what I need at the moment, and I would be willing to work for my keep."

"He's got eight children, various ages," Joel said with a grin, "Combine that fact with the stable and the horses, I'm sure they'll soon find something for you to do."

"Eight children?" Beth stared, "I shouldn't think he will have to find anything, I am sure under those circumstances I shall find it for myself."

They laughed together for a moment. One lively son was enough for Harriet, how Evans and his wife coped with eight had always been a mystery to her. Then she asked suddenly, "Did you see the report on Val and Rosa in the newspaper? We did. He looks very well, doesn't he."

"Very well," Beth agreed, trying not to give anything away. Then to change the subject, "Have you thought of doing anything to the garden at the back of the Tea Room? It would be so nice to be able to take tea on the lawn of a summer afternoon."

"That's all being taken care of," Harriet assured her. "Mr Stevens has been worrying about it for some time. I think his gardener is concerned that the weeds might cross over into his territory."

Joel grinned. "Henry Farthing is a stickler for order in the garden. He's offered to tame the Tea Room for us."

"Oh, I'm so pleased." Then a memory pushed forward from the back of Beth's mind and she added, "There is a clump of Mrs Sinkins close to one of the arches. They smelled so sweet the evening of the opening. I do hope they can be saved."

"I'll remember to mention it to him," Harriet said.

Beth hoped that she would. The bloom that she had picked at the opening had been lost, she supposed that she had dropped it on the way home, and she would have liked another to take its place.

"You will come back to the village, won't you, Beth?" Harriet asked, as she saw her out of the house and down the steps. "Neil would be lost without you."

Beth nodded, "I'll be back. I want a change of scene for a while, that's all."

"Good, then I shall write to Mr Evans as soon as I go in, and we will start to make plans."

Chapter 6

Selwyn Evans and his wife were only too pleased to help. *'The girl has something on her mind, and she is too nice a person to be left to worry on her own,'* Harriet had written. *'You helped Joel, please find a way to help Beth ...'*

So it was that a few weeks later, Beth alighted from the train at the small station and found a pony and trap waiting for her in the yard.

"Selwyn Aloysius Evans at your service, Miss Riche," Evans said, holding out his hand to help her up into her seat. "Nice to give the pony some exercise. I thought you might like it better than a noisy old motor car."

"It's perfect, Mr Evans, thank you," Beth agreed, settling down into a comfortable corner and drawing the brightly coloured travelling rug over her knees.

"Good." He clicked up the pony and they began the drive back to the farm. "It's a long way, I hope you don't get cold, but there will be a warm welcome when we get there. The whole family is waiting to meet you."

"You make me feel like an honoured guest."

"Any friend of the Meekham's is a friend of ours. How is that boy of theirs?"

"Very well, and growing more fond of horses every day. Joel is ecstatic."

"I'll bet he is. Good horses, a good family and trusted friends, no man could ask for more."

Beth had no idea what she would find when she reached the farm, but discovered that the family were not too badly off, in spite of the eight children. They lived in a massive centuries old farmhouse that had been added to from time to time during its long existence. The garden, where once the farmer's wife had kept the herbs essential for flavouring food and looking after the health of the family, was neat and tidy, a lesson for the shambles at the Tea Room.

The whole family was there, ready to greet her and make a fuss. Beth had never been a part of a large family, and found the out-pouring of affection from young and old alike overwhelming. For the girl who led a mainly solitary life, it was a strange new experience.

It was obvious from the first moment that she was welcome and would soon settle in. She had expected to stay two weeks at the most. All she had hoped for was a few days away from the village. Slowly it had dawned on her that she had made a rash decision when she turned down Val's proposal. She did feel something for him, he had been right when he suspected it. Each passing day seemed to make it more obvious. For once in her life she had been wrong. Very wrong.

The two weeks became a month. Beth learnt how Mrs Evans made Welsh Cakes and the 'speckled bread' Bara Brith, where the fruit had to be soaked overnight in tea. She made friends with the horses, fine racing horses with alert ears and impatient hooves.

It occurred to her that Evans was probably right to have such a big family. The boys worked with the horses, the girls kept the house running smoothly. Everyone seemed happy in their work, even the smaller members of the brood, and there was hardly ever a cross word.

Winter set in. The month became two months. It was bitterly cold and the fire roared up the chimney all day long. It was not the weather for her to return home, they assured her. The train journey would be unbearable. Warm, surrounded by affection, Beth needed no excuses to stay on.

Spring came, a beautiful gentle spring and she knew that soon she must leave what had come to feel like a branch of her own family. She would always think of them as her family now, for she had been treated as one of them from the day she had arrived.

It was four months since her flight from England, four delightful months with people who seemed to understand her so well and went out of their way to make her happy.

She was brown skinned from working out in all weathers with the Evans menfolk. Her long fair hair had proved an annoyance. Now it was cut short, not as short as modern fashion decreed, but to a more manageable length.

Life was very full. She still had her old people and children. Mrs Evans parents, Thomas and Marian Thomas, lived in a tiny house in the village and she often visited them along with their daughter. The Evans children were a delight to her heart. Sebastian, the oldest was trying to teach her the Welsh language, but she found it difficult and they usually ended up laughing at her mistakes. There was little time to think of home. She had been taken up in the life of a thriving farming community where everyone recognised and welcomed her.

One cloud drifted across her otherwise clear blue sky. Amid all the happiness a letter had arrived from Linda, brief but to the point. Neil's mother had died and was finally at rest.

"Poor Neil," she sighed, knowing how he must have suffered at the loss, "I wish I could have been there."

Although she tried to keep him out of her thoughts, visions of Val drifted with ghost like persistence into her picture of home. Unwillingly Beth found herself remembering the night when she had walked with him down to the village cross, and how they had talked sitting on the bottom step. Then the night of the Grand Opening and his proposal. One thing she knew. She must go back and try to find him. If he no longer felt anything for her she must at least apologise for her foolishness. If he still loved her then perhaps he would forgive her for her moment of weakness and they could find happiness together. She hoped that he would forgive her, but thought it highly unlikely. The problem was, finding the courage to go back. It would have to be soon, Val was once more on British soil but she had no doubt that he would be away again in no time.

Then the problem exploded in her face and she was forced to make her decision.

The day began just like any other. After a wet drizzly start the sun broke through and she set off for the village to visit Mr and Mrs Thomas. They were pleased to see her as she always brought news of their daughter and grandchildren.

"The newspaper, Mr Thomas," Mrs Thomas said suddenly. "Miss Riche might like to see the second page."

The old gentleman tottered off into another room and returned moments later with one of the national newspapers in his hand. "There's a story about your home village on page two," he said, giving it to Beth. "We thought that you might like to see it."

Beth flicked over the first page and was instantly drawn to a picture of the weir, their weir, with a small picture of Val Garrett set into one corner. She felt a wave of sickness come over her. The page blurred before her eyes and she screwed them up in attempt to clear her vision. It made no difference. Her hands trembled visibly as she read the headline. 'End of the Dance.' Hardly breathing she scanned the article, caught her breath and read it down properly, sure that in her haste she had misunderstood the words. There had been no mistake. It seemed that a certain big competition had come round again. As Val and his partner had missed winning by such a narrow margin before, they were now expected to come back and make good. The article was to inform dance fans that they would not be taking part, as Val had been injured when he dived into the river to save a young girl from drowning. He had managed to get her to safety. Several people who were walking nearby ran to help, but before they could haul him out he was washed into the boiling waters of the weir. When he was eventually rescued, they found that his back had been damaged.

How he lived was a miracle, but he did, and now he had left the hospital and was convalescing in London. Rosa was running the school and handling reporters. Val would speak to no one, and any strangers who managed to track him down had the door shut in their faces by an elderly relative. Beth guessed that this must be his grandmother.

"I know him," she whispered. "I know him. I know what his dancing meant to him."

"I'll make a pot of tea," Mrs Thomas murmured. "You'll be needing it I think. You're quite pale my dear."

"Poor Val," Beth stared at the picture, "He asked me to marry him once."

"He'll be needing all the help he can get now, and all the understanding." Thomas nodded to his wife, indicating that she should stay with Beth, and took the teapot into the kitchen.

"He was a fine, healthy young man," Mrs Thomas said, leaning forward to grasp Beth's hand. "The papers always make things seem worse than they are. It makes a more interesting story. He'll be on his feet in no time. You mark my words."

"I've got to go back," Beth said, as Thomas came back into the room with the tea. "I'll go and see him. Just once, that's all it will take. He will be happy and I'll be at rest for knowing it. After all, I'll be able to pick up where I left off. I'll miss the horses, but I suppose I can visit Harriet more often and I might be able to do some gardening with Mr Farthing at the Tea Room."

It took what seemed an eternity to make the arrangements, but at last Beth was on the train home. She had written to Neil so that he would know when to expect her and could have her house ready. That would be good enough until she could track Val down, then she would go to him, and throw herself on his mercy.

A family of father, mother and teenage daughter shared her compartment. They too had read the newspaper and the girl was unable to forget it.

"Well, if people will go swimming near weirs, then they must accept the consequences." The father had no sympathy for the unfortunate person.

Beth turned to face the window. She could hardly tell them to be quiet, but their words were bringing tears to her eyes.

"He wasn't swimming, and you know it. I read it to you over breakfast the other morning!" Samantha thundered, glaring savagely at her father, who remained unimpressed. "It's horrible. Poor dear, with such a gorgeous life ahead of him, and now, he's a cripple, and it's all over, and he'll never dance again " With a display of tears that would have made Delia proud, she buried her face in her mother's shoulder.

"He was very unfortunate," Mother soothed, "but he's lucky to be alive, and I expect he knows it. I doubt if he will miss his dancing all that much, he has friends, and a school to run, so there will be plenty to do."

It seemed an age before the train pulled into the station. Beth was thankful that she had told Neil she was coming. He would know what to do. First she must return to the village, and make her plans. After that she would go to the place where she had an appointment in a room with despair and misery, to banish those terrors from the darkness, and bring light into the life of the man she loved. As she reached her destination she felt new strength surging into her arms, as though she was already supporting him. She was on her way. But to what? He would not see anyone, perhaps he would not want to see her.

The thought stabbed rapier like into her heart, and for a moment it almost seemed to stand still. It would be ironical if now, when she wanted him so much, he had grown to hate her.

A welcome sight met her eyes. Neil Haily was half way down the platform to greet her. He looked different, older, little wispy bits of white flecked his lush blond hair. She had enjoyed herself on the farm and until now had flourished. I her absence Neil had suffered the loss of the invalid mother who he had loved and cherished for so long.

He came forward the moment he saw her, and opened the carriage door. His hand gripped hers, such a beautiful hand, so strong and yet so tender, "Welcome home, Beth," he said, "I've got a taxi outside. I'm taking you back to our place. Lin has a bed ready. We want you to stay with us tonight."

Overwhelmed by gratitude, Beth could only say, "I asked you to open my house."

They pushed through the crowd at the barrier, all waving to friends who had come off the train. How like Neil, she thought, to be right there on the platform, even though it was so small that hardly anyone else had bothered.

"We didn't want you to be alone for the first night," he replied softly.

Chapter 7

Linda greeted her friend warmly, "I'll make a cup of tea," she offered, and went into the kitchen.

"Neil, what has happened to Val?" Beth turned suddenly in her chair, "They say that he has changed."

"Yes, he has changed."

"How?"

"He has become resentful and disagreeable."

"What, Val?"

"Yes, Val. In hospital he was snapping and snarling all the time, giving the nurses no rest day or night. If you ask me, they only discharged him because they had had enough."

"How he must have suffered."

"But there was no need to make other's lives hell because of it."

"Is there no hope for the man we all knew?"

Neil's eyes were pensive, "No hope, Beth?" he questioned. "I wouldn't say that there was no hope. He has still got his life. He had the sense to hold onto that."

Beth fought back her emotions. It was a hard battle. She was tired out, and would have wilted away in a flood of tears if Neil had not been there, "I love him, Neil, is it too late?"

"Love never comes ... too late ... Beth," he answered, taking her hand and giving it a squeeze, "It's the kind of love that matters."

Linda brought the tea and there was silence for a while as Beth drank it. That done she lay back in the armchair, the empty teacup on the table beside her, dark shadows threatening to close her tired eyes.

Neil stood before her on the hearthrug, one hand on the mantle shelf, the other in his pocket, his foot resting on the fender. He was looking at her intently, wondering how much more she could take.

Of all the people who fluttered round Val when the accident first happened, only two remained constant, himself and Melody. Slowly he told her everything he had seen and heard. Told it with what she thought was brutal clarity, until at last unable to stand any more, she burst into tears.

He said nothing but waited until she dried her eyes.

Linda kept well out the way, she had wept enough of late. She sat baby Jenny her knee and folded her alms about her, thankful that the sweetest woman in the village had at least been able to hold her grandchild in her arms during those last few days. Neil had almost lived at the hospital towards the end. No one questioned his need to be there. The children at the school were quiet and subdued, even the dreadful Brakes boy. All seemed to be sharing his grief.

Then came the dreadful night when he returned home early. He said little, but his strong hands spoke for him, and she knew that although his eyes could never weep tears his heart was weeping profusely. So they had clung together in the darkness and she had kissed those beautiful hands, and prayed that in time the pain would be eased.

Downstairs, Neil began speaking again.

"I wish I could have been there," he was saying. "I can swim as well as the next man, better than most," and it was no idle boast so why should he be ashamed of saying so. "I might have managed to save him, or help him save himself."

"And have two of you hurt? No, Neil, these things must happen. But why? What has Val done to be cut down so?"

Neil shook his head and fiddled with the little blue and white ornaments on the mantle. "I wish I knew. His life seemed so full. He had everything. Since he stayed with Rosa his progress was rapid. Perhaps that's why it's come as such a shock … they tell me the first thing he did when he got home was asked for his dancing shoes."

"I remember they were all hand made. What pride he used to take in them."

"I don't think he'll wear them again."

"Why do you save that?"

"Because he flung them in the fireplace. It took all of Melody's patience and a scolding from his grandmother to stop him having them put in the dustbin."

Beth sighed. "What are his plans, Neil, do you know?"

He shook his head. "He has none."

"None at all?"

"When a man has such an upset in life, he generally turns to his wife, his religion, or a friend. Val has no wife. The one person who could have been close to him at all times is missing."

"And his religion?"

"Lost in the whirling waters of the weir."

"But he has you, and Melody."

"He won't talk to Melody about … personal things."

She screwed up her eyes and rubbed them in a vain attempt to stop them smarting. "Will he talk to you?"

There was no answer. When she looked up Neil was staring out the window above her head.

"We share one thing in common," he said at last. "Or at least, I once thought we did."

"What was that, can you tell me?"

He looked down at her gravely solemn, and shook his head. "No woman should know the secrets of a man's mind, let alone the minds of two men. That's a great difference between us, women share their secrets, a man takes them like staves in his heart, to the grave itself."

She put out her hand to him. "Don't, Neil, you're frightening me."

His smile was sad, and once more he looked away. "When they let him out of hospital they sent a nurse with him. A man of course. No woman could support him, even when he has lost so much weight." Then as she drew a sharp breath, "it's best you know that. He is no longer Harriet's Greek God."

Clinking sounds came from the kitchen, Linda was getting the tea. They both looked at the pretty blue and white china clock, which matched the ornaments on the mantle shelf.

"I'll tell her you're not ready," he said.

"No," Beth rolled her head sleepily in the chair. "I'll have a bite to eat, and then I'll be ready to rest."

"Good. You need sleep more than any-thing else at the moment."

Her smile was wistful, but genuine. "You're wrong, Neil, it's food I need most. I haven't had anything for ages."

It was quite like old times, sitting in the bright spacious kitchen with Linda and Neil. Everything seemed the same, the colour scheme, the china, even the teapot. Only the chair on the fourth side of the table remained empty. How she wished that she could have been there with them, and tried her best the way they were trying for her now.

She ate little, managed a cup of tea and one of Linda's small cakes. Then for a moment she closed her eyes.

The next thing she knew, firm hands were on her, and she could hear Neil saying quietly, "Open the door, love, she's out on her feet."

She felt him help her from the chair, and guide her while Linda led the way and opened the door of the spare room. Then she was sinking down on to something soft, and those same firm hands removed her shoes. Free from them her tired feet relaxed. A cover was thrown over her and she slept.

It was morning when Beth awoke. Sunday morning in her own village, and the birds were singing in the fresh green garden beyond the lattice window.

Someone was on the landing outside. With a gentle tap on the door Linda came in.

Beth sat up and stretched. "You shouldn't have let me sleep in my clothes all night," she murmured, still drowsy.

"Don't be silly, Neil said you had to rest, so we left you. I'm getting breakfast if you would like to come down."

"Let me wash first."

As quickly and she could, Beth went to the bathroom, stripped and splashed herself with cold water. Refreshed, she dressed in clean clothes taken from her case, and went downstairs.

Breakfast in the Hailey household was a simple meal consisting of toast and marmalade and enough coffee to bath in. They passed the morning quietly all talking together in the sunny garden with Jenny scampering about the lawn.

At ten forty five Neil looked at his watch. "Coming to church, Beth?"

She paused for a moment before saying, "Yes, I'd like to."

"Get your hat, then, we must start. I prefer to walk, unless it's raining."

They went slowly down the street together. Linda stayed behind. She usually went to evensong, when baby Jenny was tucked up in bed and Neil could stand guard.

People turned and nodded at Beth from time to time. She smiled in return but spoke to no one.

Melody waved to them from her upstairs

window, her face lighting up when she saw who Neil had on his arm.

Even the calmness of the old grey stone building, with its heavy wood beams and brightly lit alter could not still her fears. The psalm was the twenty third, and she remembered what Neil had said the afternoon before. What had happened back there at the weir?

Beth shuddered. She remembered the china cup she had broken when he had visited her on the night of the Grand Opening. She has shattered his cup then, and gone on later to shatter his life later. If she had trusted his judgment he might have taken more care. The china cup had been repaired, in a fashion, but the cup of a man's soul was harder to mend.

Chapter 8

The service over they began to walk home.

"Neil, where did I go wrong?" she asked.

"How can I say?" He stopped walking as they approached the patch of green in the centre of the village, with the grey Celtic cross, and followed her gaze towards the monument. "I only know part of the story."

"Then I must tell you the rest."

They sat on a rustic seat near to the cross. Suddenly Beth was tense, her hands clasped tightly in her lap, her eyes on the bottom step where she had sat with Val. Neil leaned back against the frame of the seat, one knee crossed over the other, one elbow on the wooden arm, his eyes on the woman who was about to trust him with the secrets of her heart. A silence followed, a heavy silence, which she could not find the strength to break and he did not try.

Then with a deep sigh she said, "I'll tell you everything as it happened. Perhaps that way you will understand."

Neil nodded. "Very well, and don't be afraid, your secrets are safe with me."

"Oh, Neil, you know better than anyone else what my life has been. I was an orphan, I had to trust to strangers with my upbringing. Though they tried, I never felt that I was really wanted. All that time, even into adult life I needed someone to love and be loved by, but that someone never came."

Her companion turned his head, and watched two old men leaning on their walking sticks as they wove their wobbly way out of the churchyard in the direction of the public house.

"I have been cared about and I have cared deeply about people, but I have never loved … do you follow me, Neil?"

He looked much older, much thinner, she thought, as he answered thickly, "I follow you."

"I made friends easily during the War. I had reasons to talk to people and they had cause to speak to me. The old folk became like the grandparents I had never known."

Her friend smiled. He knew well enough how the elderly members of their community had valued her visits. "You helped some of them more than you realize. Old they may be, but they still had their own, sometimes very personal, reasons to be interested in what was happening. Had you not read the newspapers to them they would have had to wait who knows how long to hear."

"I remember Val from the old days. He was a very earnest young man, with a dream of making a living with the skill in his feet. How people laughed, but I think even then I knew that he could do it." She paused, but Neil would not break into her thoughts. "I suppose I was interested in him, because we were so much alike. Our parents had both died. At least he still had a grandmother. Then came the evening of the Grand Opening and we danced together ..." It had been easy thinking things over in her our own mind. Now, as she tried to put her feelings into words they seemed such poor things, conveying so little of what she felt. The look in Neil's eyes did little to help. Somehow it made her feel smaller and more helpless.

A smile twitched at the corners of his mouth. She had enjoyed dancing with Val Garrett. He had thought it then, and now, when she spoke of it her eyes flashed. Yes, she had enjoyed it.

"I thought he was being silly and mistaking me for just another in the long line of dance partners. It was as simple as that. I didn't dream that he was in love with me. How could I? All those beautiful girls he danced with. How could I know that they meant nothing to him, that he had found what he wanted in me?" His words came back to her, 'I'm asking you. Are you doubting my judgment?' and she wished with all her heart that she had trusted him. "While we danced he had seen something in me that stole his heart. I don't know what it was or if it really exists. For him it did, and I didn't know."

"It exists," Neil answered. The vision had been his early in life when he had watched her as a child playing with her dolls, caring for them with a devotion she would be capable of giving a man and his children in later years. His only regret was that the love was not for him. She treated him as a friend, and he would ask for no more.

"I'm glad someone else has seen it. If you say it's there then it must be true. I remember there was some gossip about him and Rosa. I wanted him to put an end to it. When he said that he intended to marry soon, I never felt in the least bit jealous." She broke off her words cut short by a sudden catching of her breath.

Neil sighed deeply and closed his eyes, she was crying again. He wanted above all things to fold her in his arms and make it better, but that could not be, and so he waited patiently in silence.

It was only a moment before she continued. "The personal things I can't tell you, but I can say this, he told me of his love for one woman alone. I listened, and my heart began to turn as though a knife were in it. I didn't hate the girl, but I did wish for a moment that it could have been me. Then he told me that I *was* the one he wanted to marry." Her eyes were wide as she turned to him. "I didn't know what to do, Neil, he wanted me for his wife."

Neil linked his hands together, he knew they were trembling and didn't want her to see. "Was that so terrible?"

"I couldn't believe it. How could a man who loved beautiful things be proposing to me? Me, Neil," her voice rose in bewilderment, "all five foot six and a half inches of me, with big feet, big hands and …"

"A big heart, which he had seen."

She stopped and stared into his clear blue eyes. Was it true? Could she, the ugly duckling, be a swan at heart? She continued in a low voice. "I asked for time to think about it and he said he would expect an answer the next day. Every time I thought of it I wanted to say 'yes,' but then I would think of those beautiful girls he would have to dance with. What would people say? Would I grow up old and jealous?"

"Poor Beth, the moment of truth. Go on."

"I remember everything so clearly. I sat on the fence and he leaned across the style. It was so beautiful. He asked for my answer and I refused him."

There was a long silence. Neil understood only too well what Val Garrett had felt. Eventually he spoke, not looking up, not daring to meet her eyes. "Why, Beth?"

"It seemed to be right at the time. Perhaps I'd not fallen in love then. I was fond of him, but when it came to marriage I thought only of what he would be tied to for the rest of his life, and what he could have if he tried."

Neil studied a little pink stone by his foot.

"It is seldom a matter of choice with us," he said when he could trust his voice to stay calm "What we could have bears no weight against what we want."

"As an old and dear friend, Neil, tell me if I did right?"

"I'm no judge of morals. You should ask the vicar."

"I can't talk to anyone else."

"Then what can I say?" He shook his head sadly. "Can I say that when you had the chance to be everything to this man, you turned the offer down because you were afraid of what the future would bring? Can I say that, Beth?"

"I wasn't afraid!"

"You were afraid that you would be jealous of his beautiful partners, or so you have told me. Your fear panicked you into making a rash decision. Are you sure it isn't guilt that is driving you into a second?"

"Neil, don't!"

"My dear girl, you must take some chances in life. If you marry a person you take them for better or worse. It's there in your vows. No outsider can break up a truly devoted couple, because they will know each other too well for outside interference to make any difference. You threw his offer in his face because you were afraid …"

"Stop it, Neil! Don't be cruel!"

Neil's eyes flashed. "Yesterday I said that I didn't know why he let himself be swept away. I thought he had a full cup. I was wrong, I see that now. That cup had been shattered by the woman he believed to be so strong."

"Neil, you don't know what it's like … the pain …" she bit off the words and put out her hand to touch his white flecked hair, but he jerked his head away. "I'm sorry, I'm hurting you now. I'm not as good a person as everyone thinks."

"Beth, you deserved every moment of torment for breaking his heart. You need it too, so that you can be stung into opening your eyes."

She drew her big hands down her face drying her tears. "I know, you've made me understand."

"You let a moment of panic come between you and what could have been yours." He thought for a moment, his eyes on the top off the cross. "Val is like a princess in one of my sons storybooks. She would eat nothing but cakes until the baker gave her so many she made herself sick. Then she was glad of simple bread and butter." He smiled. "Don't you see it, Beth, Val danced with so many cakes he longed for something wholesome and not sticky."

"Dear God. What have I done?"

"What indeed. When I think of the way he has carried on, the hours of practice, the sweat of performances. He reached the top, but it was lonely there. His chance of released came and he took it. Perhaps it was a rash decision. Perhaps you are both to blame, for now he is crippled and you are …"

"Desolate."

"Quite."

Beth began to realize that things were not going to be as easy as she had at first thought. The man she had come to for help seemed harder than she had expected. "I want to see him," she said suddenly.

Neil studied a fingernail. "Yes, I expect you do. However I don't think he will want to see you."

"But I've got to be there. It's the only

place in the world for me."

"I agree. Having said that, once there what could you do?"

"Oh, Neil," she took one of his hands in both her own, and the look in her eyes was of such tenderness that he could not meet it. "I would know what to do."

"Would you?" He removed his hand, and standing moved away from her. For a moment his back was all she could see. Then he turned slowly. "You've got to see things from his side. Perhaps that is where I can help you the most."

"Please try."

"You must see the difference between you. If a man's feelings have been hurt the wound is often deep and untreatable. When he had a sure future ahead of him he was not good enough for you …" he held up his hand to curb the protest he could see forming on her lips. "That is what he is going to think. But now he may never lead a normal life again, you come back and want to be with him. Will he be just another child or sick dog to you?"

"He loves me …"

"Oh, yes, I know. But think of what it

would be like knowing the one you loved only came back when you needed pushing round like a sick animal."

"If he loves me, won't he want me there in any case?"

"He had the strength to put that love from him once," Neil reminded her. "I could not have done it. If I had spoken of love and you had turned me down, I could not have left you. We would probably have both ended up in trouble. But there you are, it only goes to show how strong he can be."

"Neil, how can I make him see that I wanted to come back before I heard of the accident? He would never believe that I was away all those months and had not heard, but you know yourself, the Welsh valleys can be very remote."

Neil Hailey drew a deep shuddering breath. "I believe you. There is no need to try convincing me." He was already forming a plan. "Beth, how strong are you, in courage, I mean? Could you visit his house and not see him? Could you live nearby and never be able to say what you want to say?"

Her eyes widened. "Neil, what you are asking me to do?"

"You want to serve him, Beth, then serve him you shall. If you find a chance, then take it, but you will only have a few weeks. If you have failed you must come back. Do you understand?"

"I understand what you are saying, but I don't understand what you mean."

He took a letter from his pocket. "This is from his companion, a word I use more freely than nurse, because Freddie Delgado has become more friend than medical assistant. Val has kept his tie with the village. He wondered if I knew of a young lady who would like to go up there for a working holiday, to help his grandmother. The old lady had no problem when Val was on his feet, more away than he was at home, but now he is there and … unsociable, she is finding it hard."

"Does he still see Rosa?"

"She takes care of the business. I hear it is doing very well. She goes there often, supposedly on business. Granny tells me it's to see Fred, they appear to be at the 'walking out together' stage."

Beth hesitated, but only for a moment, before replying. "It seems a good plan." She smiled a little uncertainly and stood up. "I will put myself in your hands."

"And nowhere could you be safer," he said with a sigh.

Chapter 9

The days leading up to Beth's departure for London seemed to drag. Once she was on the train and heading for the city it suddenly seemed that there had been no time at all to prepare for what was to come.

Rosa came hurrying to the door of the big white house to let her in.

They looked, at each other for a moment, then Rosa said, "Hello, Beth, I know all about it."

"Neil?" Beth's heart beat thankfully, glad there was no explaining to do.

"He put everything in the letter when he asked if you might come to stay."

"He is very thorough."

"Yes, dear, he is," and there was a touch of pity in Rosa's voice.

"I know now that I'm in love with Val," Beth murmured very low. "I should never have refused him."

"So I understand. Isn't it a bind, I love that handsome great Italian over the fence, so I know what it's like."

"Over the fence?" Beth was intrigued.

"Didn't Neil tell you Val bought the house that backs onto this one? He intended to have a gate made joining the two properties together. It never came about. He's cut himself off from the world and when I want to go there I have to go all round the houses." Then with a friend's interest, "When it first happened he wouldn't allow us to even speak your name, but later if we dropped a few words in your favour he let it pass. Perhaps there is a chance of your success."

"Oh, Rosa, I hope so."

Beth had been given a spacious airy room at the back of the house. Its large windows gave a splendid view of the compact, beautifully styled garden, the fence, the garden of the house backing it and the house itself.

"I must remember not to go too close to the windows," Beth said, stepping back a pace. "I don't want Val to see me before we are ready."

"He won't see you," her friend sighed.

"But from the garden …"

"He doesn't come into the garden. He stays in his room on the second floor most of the time. He has never even come down the stairs."

"But ... surely if he has someone to help him ..."

"He has rejected everything, Beth. He doesn't want to see or be seen. You're going to have your work cut out just getting him down the stairs. To have him out in the garden where he might see you ... at the moment I would say that's impossible."

"All because I doubted his judgement." Beth sat down on her bed, her own legs suddenly weak with the horror of what she had caused.

"It was the weir that crippled him."

"The water crippled his body, my stupidity crippled his mind. He was so happy the night of Harriett's Grand Opening ... so happy."

There was a pause, and then Rosa said, "Come and see the room upstairs. Come on, I'll show you."

Beth followed slowly behind her sprightly dark haired companion as they mounted the stairs to the very top of the house. She did not know what awaited them there, and as she neared the door her heart began to thump with uneasy expectancy.

Rosa pushed the door open and they went inside. It was dark, the curtains being drawn, and she swiftly drew them aside.

"Well, Beth, how do you like it?"

Beth looked about her awe struck, "Beautiful," she said.

"Exactly! This is where all the hard work was done."

It was a splendid place. The floor was bare and polished to a glass like shine. The walls were dark green picked out here and there with a lush yellow border. Between these panels were large mirrors, bright and shining like the hopes of the two young people who had built the room. At one end stood a piano, a gramophone, and a couple of chairs. The other end was taken up by a massive wardrobe and three rows of shelves, on which winked and sparkled the trophies they had gained in their short but brilliant career.

Rosa flung open the wardrobe door, and immediately the empty space was filled with yards of satin and tulle, which seemed in a hurry to get out for an airing. She sorted through the dresses, before selecting a green one. "I wore this in Paris," she said, holding it up to her shoulders.

"Oh, what a waste," Beth touched the lovely dress, "Why don't you use them? You could find another partner, Val wouldn't mind."

"My dear, it shows just how little you understand," and Rosa put the dress back quickly, "Val and I were thunder and lightning, we went together. Separated, I'm afraid neither of us would cause such alarm. He was the brilliant one. If you had ever danced with him in a competition you would have known the inferior feeling he gave. He didn't mean it, poor dear, but he was so clever," she shrugged, "And now it's come to this. Look at these beautiful things." She took up one of the trophies, a silver statuette of a couple dancing, "I used to think some of them were hideous, but this is divine. Oh Beth, perhaps it happened for a reason. A man shouldn't sell his soul to anything, should he?"

"I don't think so."

"Val did. He lived to dance. When you turned him down it was worse than ever."

"You know all about it?"

"Freddy. Oh hell! I don't think Val loved anything, not even you as much as this lot.

Now it's all been taken from him," she laughed brokenly, "What for? The idiot could have saved himself, he's a damned good swimmer. Instead he didn't try. Neil told me that you were coming back to him. God, if he'd waited ..." and she sank into one of the chairs in a flood of tears.

The next morning Beth took her courage in both hands and made her way around the houses to begin her mission. A gate in the fence would have been nice. It was quite a long street and they were more or less in the middle of it.

For a while she stood on the grey gravel path, looking at the tall white painted building wondering how one elderly woman kept it in order.

A man appeared at an upstairs window. A tall man, handsome and Italian. He waved, and disappeared almost instantly from view.

Moments later the door opened and he was in the entrance smiling a welcome and saying "Come in, Miss Burke. It's very good of you to offer your assistance."

"Thank you, Mr ..."

"Delgado. I help look after Mr. Garrett."

He held out his hand and gave hers a shattering squeeze.

"I'm only too happy to be here," she murmured, entering through the heavy oak door into the cool hall. So this was Val's home. She looked round, loving it instantly because it was his.

"Mrs. Drummond is in the living room," Freddy indicated the room opposite them with a wave of his hand. "Perhaps you would like to meet her."

"If I am to help with a spring clean, then I really think I should," Beth replied. She was shaking already. How would she manage? Here she was, miles away from home, surrounded by strangers and pretending to be someone she was not. Would Mrs Drummond see through her? What about Val? Would she see him before she was ready and be sent away in disgrace?

The old lady was on a chair dusting the ledges of the heavy window frame when she entered.

Her hand went out at once to help her but it was ignored. Granny Drummond may be as old as the hills, white capped and whether beaten like them, but she was still a tough highland lassie at heart.

"Miss Burke?" she asked, eventually coming down and folding her duster.

"Betty, Mrs. Drummond," Beth answered.

"Yes, I see," Catherine Drummond stood by the window very much the mistress of the house. "So you have come … Betty … Burke."

"Yes." This was awful. From the moment she had entered the room the old lady's manner had seemed strange and suspicious.

There was another long pause. Once more she was looked over, then, "It's nice to have you, Miss Burke."

"Thank you."

"My grandson likes to keep his contact with the village, you know."

"Mr. Haley told me." Even thinking of him made her feel better. He had taken her to the train and she remembered his warm touch the moment before the door closed between them. 'Go to your destiny, Beth,' he had said. 'Go, and don't be afraid.'

"He's a nice young man," Mrs. Drummond continued.

"He is, very nice."

"And clever, *oh so very, very, clever.*"

Granny nodded wisely. "He gets on well with my grandson. I expect he has told you how he has shut the door on the world and will not see anyone."

"Mr. Haily has explained the situation in full detail."

"They thought this idea up between them, to give me a hand." Her back straightened. "Not that I need it, you understand."

"I'll do only what you ask."

The tension between them seemed to relax a little. "Perhaps Mr Delgado will go and tell Mr. Garrett that you have arrived."

"At once, Mrs Drummond," and Freddy left closing the door noiselessly behind him.

Granny sighed, "My grandson may be master of the house, but you will not see him," she said. "Unfortunately since his accident he has become a recluse and he will seldom leave his room. A great shame, a pretty face such as yours might have aroused his interest in life once more."

"Oh, I would hardly say that I was pretty," Beth laughed self-consciously.

"You're a fine, strong young lass with a good honest way about you. No man has any right to ask for more," Granny snapped somewhat sharply. "Now, there are things that need to be lifted off the high shelves in the scullery and I want to begin cleaning them."

"Yes, Mrs Drummond." Beth smiled knowing that in spite of the old lady's strange manner she had been accepted. Of course she realized that this was the easy part. Granny had never seen her before. Any meeting with Val would be different.

After a few seconds, in which she nearly packed her case and ran, Beth was ready to face the task ahead. Neil had sent her, and Neil was never wrong. Head high she followed the old lady into the scullery there to begin the late spring cleaning.

In no time at all Beth was on a chair lifting jars, pans and containers from the high shelf that ran around the four walls of the room. Carefully she handed them down to the old lady who stacked them on a table ready to be washed.

"Senseless to have all these things," Granny Drummond commented, depositing a large copper jam pan on the table with a 'thunk.' "We hardly ever use them. The only time they come down is when they are washed."

"I'm afraid I keep things for the kitchen that I don't really need," Beth confessed. "Some of them are too pretty to throw away. Some have been handed down the family. I always think that one day I may need them."

On leaving the pair to get on with their work, Freddy had left the door wide open. As they talked, their voices drifted out into the hall and up the stairs.

Val had been trying to look interested in a book he was supposed to be reading. He was bored, but the sound of the voices below soon drew his attention. He frowned. "What did you say the girl's name was?"

"Miss Burke," Freddy replied calmly, not lifting his eyes from his own book.

"Are you sure?"

"You saw Mr Haily's letter."

"Yes, I know … but …"

"But?" Freddy turned a page and gave the appearance of continuing to read. In fact his attention never left his patient for one moment. Just a few words from the visitor and Val was interested. Something was going on here that he had not expected. Even lovely

Rosa did not have that effect.

"What does she look like?"

"In what particular way?"

"Oh, for goodness sake, man! Is she tall, or short, what colour hair does she have?"

"Why don't you go down and find out, or if you think that would be too much for you at the minute, ask her to come up here."

Val glared at his companion. He was fast losing his patience. "Is she tall or short?"

"Of middle height, I would say." The reply told everything and at the same time, nothing.

"Is she thin? Fat?"

"Slender. Used to working out of doors, I would say. She already has a healthy tan."

"Oh." That didn't sound right. It was Beth's voice, but it could not be Beth speaking. It was well into summer before her skin began to tan.

Silence for a moment, then, "How about her hair. What colour is it?"

"Pale."

Beth's hair was light mousey, that might pass as pale.

"Long or short?"

"Short."

Well, that was it then. As long as he had known her, Beth had boasted masses of long hair which she always wore screwed up in a hideous bun on top of her head. How he had wanted to snatch out the pins and watch it fall onto her shoulders. A face like hers needed to be framed by hair. Pulled back as she had it she looked dreadful. Perhaps it was her only fault. The girl really had no sense of style at all.

The talking went on. It was confusing and annoying. Freddy had answered all of his questions, but in a way that they told very little about the owner of the voice. Val began to make plans.

Beth and Granny stopped their work at midday for a quick lunch. That over they continued for another hour before the old lady sent her companion home. Tomorrow, they had decided, they would attack the entrance hall, and in particular the space under the stairs.

Chapter 10

Rosa wanted to know everything that had happened and was disappointed when she heard there had been no contact between Beth and Val.

"I made sure that I talked rather loudly in the hope that he would hear me," her guest said, "but nothing happened."

Rosa shrugged and threw out her hands in a helpless gesture. "I suppose we can't expect instant results," she sighed. "I was hoping ... but ... well, we must see what tomorrow brings."

'Tomorrow' saw Beth at the Garrett residence bright and early. Granny was delighted.

"You see the problem, Miss Burke," the old lady said, pointing to the large cabinet that was fitted tightly under the stairs. "I can't get in there to dust it properly and it's unhealthy. It used to shine once. Pride and joy in my cottage. When Valentine brought me to London we could find no place for it.

There they put it, and there it has stayed. *Gathering dust!"*

"Perhaps Mr Delgado could lever it out a little," Beth suggested, regarding the heavy piece of furniture with loving eyes. To her it was beautiful, even dusty, and she longed to buff it up and get a shine on it once more.

"It took two strong men to get it in there, and it will take two strong men to get it out!" Granny replied. "All I ask is that you get yourself in what space they have left at the side, and do what you can with the duster."

Beth heaved a sigh and pushed at her sleeves. She was going to war, with a beautiful mahogany cabinet, and she had no doubts what so ever as to who the winner would be.

Upstairs Val listened intently to the voices as they drifted up from below.

"Granny is complaining about her cabinet again," he said casting his eyes heavenward. "I wish to goodness it had fallen off the van on the way down. It doesn't fit in anywhere here, only under the stairs."

"Gathering dust …" Freddy added with a grin.

"As you say." A moment of thought, then Val said, "Push me out onto the landing, will you. I'd like to give the girl a word of encouragement."

Freddy said nothing, just did as he was told.

Beth was in the act of crawling under the stairs when the pair came to the ornate rail that edged the landing.

"She has one nice ankle at least," Freddy remarked, leaning over to watch the activity below.

Val smiled softly. From a seated position he had not seen the ankle. He wished he had. "I knew someone with nice ankles once," he said softly. "She was most embarrassed when she knew that I had noticed them."

"Gentlemen do not comment on ladies ankles," his companion reminded him. "Well, not unless it is to another gentleman. Never to the lady in question."

"It was only a professional interest that drew my attention, that time. Afterwards I must confess …" Then he edged an inch closer to the stair rail. "Please forgive me not coming down, Miss Burke," he called. "I am not the man I was, and you must understand that I have no wish to be gawped at now. I am glad you're here, you will doubtless be of great assistance to my grandmother."

"I don't need help," the old lady muttered, "only with you, and I have Mr. Delgado for that."

"And he bullies me as much as you do."

"Who wouldn't bully you?" his grandmother retorted savagely. "When they let you out of hospital they said you were ready to start a new life."

"New but restricted."

"Not this restricted. If you ask me your brain was hurt at the same time as your back, and they haven't found out!"

Beth's voice came muffled but distinct from under the stairs, "Are you sure it wasn't his pride?"

Realizing that he was not going to see anything, Val had been about to trundle back to his room. He stopped suddenly, causing Freddy to bump into his chair and say something sharp in Italian. "What did you say your name was, girl?" he demanded.

"Miss Burke," Gran snapped airily. "She's the young lady Mr Haily found at a loose end and needing something to occupy her mind."

"Are you sure?" Val's tone was uncertain. "Dammit, come out from under the stairs and let me see you, girl!"

"I'm afraid that's impossible, sir," Beth replied catching her breath. "I have just crawled behind the furniture. It wasn't easy and I don't want to have to do it again."

Granny grunted her displeasure. "If all you can do is delay us in our work then I suggest you return to your room, boy," she scolded. "Miss Burke is quite right. It's a very tight corner and she is unlikely to want to push her way back into it once she is out." Then she added, "And I want that corner cleaned. *It's all dust!*"

"Very well, Granny," Val replied, "I'll let you get on, only don't work the poor girl too hard. Neil will never forgive me if I let you work her down to skin and bone."

"No chance of that with this lass," Granny countered. "She's a fine young girl and I have a feeling that we will get along well."

"I hope that doesn't mean that you are going to teach her to bully me like you do!"

"I don't bully …"

"Oh not much!"

"… I just tell the truth."

Trying to force herself deeper into the recess behind the chest Beth bumped her head and said, "Ow!"

"There!" Granny snapped. "Now look what's happened! Stop distracting us and go back to your sulking."

This time Val did retreat and they heard the door click shut behind him.

"As if I would bully an invalid," Granny mumbled.

Beth extricated herself from the confined space behind the cabinet, dust on her shoulder and her hair awry.

"I'm sure you wouldn't bully *an invalid,* Mrs Drummond," she said, "but someone who has given up trying must be … encouraged to go on."

Granny looked at her sternly for a moment, nodded and said. "Your hair is untidy, there is a mirror on the wall by the door."

Val was unusually quiet that evening. At last he said, "I think perhaps I would like to move downstairs for a while. I'm tired of the same view from the window. Now the weather is improving it would be nice to be able to go out onto the terrace."

"It would be nice if you could go up and down the stairs, then you wouldn't be restricted to one floor," Freddy replied calmly.

"Yes, it would be nice. Unfortunately it isn't going to happen," Val sighed. "I'd have to be carried, and no one is going to do that."

"If you could take the weight on your legs, one shoulder and the stair rail would help."

Val made no reply. He was beginning to dream again, the tantalizing dream that he could walk. After being stuck for so long in one room even the threat of crutches would be bearable if they would help him move about again. No one need see the once brilliant ballroom dancer hopping about in the privacy of his own back garden. It was a dream, though, he was convinced of that. He would never stand on his own two feet again.

Granny insisted that they should wait until the weekend when Neil was due to visit. She was very firm on the subject and would not listen to any objections.

"He can help bring you down," she said sharply. "You can't expect a woman to do that."

"You can't expect Neil to either, Gran," Val replied softly. "He inherited his mother's heart condition and he isn't strong. We don't want to deprive the village school of the best teacher it has ever known."

"Then he can keep you occupied while the rest of us do the work."

When Granny spoke like that even sulking grandsons gave way, and Val spun about to stare out of the window across the garden, over the fence and towards the building that had once been the scene of so much activity. If he was on the ground floor he could have a gate made in the fence as he had intended and perhaps sometimes when no one was about he could go and see Rosa. Rosa did not bully like Granny or try to push him into doing more than he wanted to like Freddy. Yes, it would be nice to escape to Rosa sometimes, and perhaps, if Miss Burke was still there he might eventually get to meet the girl.

Saturday morning dawned bright and clear. There was quite a bit of furniture to be moved from one floor to the other and Granny enlisted the aid of two burly men who lived nearby. Val insisted on being the first bit of furniture to be brought down, and once on the ground floor trundled merrily about getting in everyone's way. In desperation Freddy ignored his protests, wheeled him out onto the terrace, and left him there. So it was that he missed Beth's arrival. Wheeling aimlessly up and down, once more getting used to what fresh air smelt like, he paused by the window of the room that was soon to be his domain. A ladder was leaning up against the window on the inside of the room, a long ladder, and a young woman was standing near the top of it.

"Hello," he called, "Is that Miss Burke up there? Sorry I can't see your face, only your ankles. They are nice ankles, by the way."

The ladder wobbled a fraction as the person descended a couple of rungs, but still not enough to see her properly.

"I'm sorry I can't come down, Mr Garrett," she said. "Granny has insisted that the curtain needed a small repair, and it's easier to do it while it is still hanging. I have no desire to bring everything down, and then have to take it back up again."

"Granny is working you very hard, Miss Burke."

"I'm used to hard work, Mr Garrett, besides …"

"Besides?"

"It keeps my mind off other things."

"Such as?" A cotton reel dropped with a thump to the carpet. "I say, was that supposed to happen? It's not the one you are using, is it?"

"It's not the one." *It was* the one, but there was no way in which Beth was coming down to retrieve it.

"Good. What is repairing my curtain keeping your mind off of, Miss Burke? Can you tell me?"

"I've … There's a man …"

"Ah. He's pursuing you and you don't want him to."

Rather the other way about, Beth thought as she snipped at her thread with a pair of small, viciously pointed scissors. "We have had a falling out."

"Have you tried to make up?"

"He won't see me."

"Do you have a friend who could plead your case for you?"

Beth hesitated, "Someone has already tried to help, even he failed."

"Then forget him. There must be plenty of other men who would leap at the chance."

"I love him, Mr Garrett," and she hoped he would not hear the tears in her voice as she spoke. "I know he loved me once. I'm hoping that in time he will forget what happened and listen to me again."

"But if he won't see reason ..."

"He must be given time."

Val nodded slowly. "I'm glad you've told me. You see, I have trodden on similar ground. I found the one person in the world I could love, and she turned me down. I go on hoping that one day everything will be all right, and perhaps I will find someone else, but all the time I know that any other partner would only be second best."

"Life can be very difficult at times," Betty Burke said with a sigh.

"Very," he agreed, then, "Did he really love you, this unreasonable man? If he loved you, surely he would let you come back to him, no matter what you have done."

"He loved me then, but I believe I killed all the love that was in him."

"Love is not killed that easily," Val replied quickly, "It rises, like the Phoenix from the flames of life. Don't give up. Waken that love in him, Miss Burke, don't let it die."

"If only I could," it was a cry from the very bottom of her heart, and she put up a hurried hand to brush away the tears.

"Does he know you have seen your blunder?" Val went on, thinking of Beth, and wishing that he could have her, even if it was up a ladder on the other side of the window, saying the things this stranger was saying.

"I think under the present circumstances he wouldn't listen," she sniffed hard, "I suppose I should make him see me, but it would be the beginning or end, and I can't face the end yet."

"You poor girl," Val understood only too well, and saw in her predicament his own, "Promise me something."

"If it isn't too difficult," and she waited, wondering what he would say.

"I have come through troubled waters too. I thought that if I gave myself whole heartedly to my career I could forget her. It is not true. Hard work can dull the wound, but scar tissues are easily broken, and soon you start to bleed again. In one of these times I had a chance of death. I had never contemplated suicide, but in a flash it seemed the only way to escape. So I tried to die. Now I have no woman, no life in my legs and no career."

"You asked me to promise something, Mr Garrett."

"I want you to swear that you will never try to take your life. I believe that if there is a God up there, He makes a practical joke of us who want to throw in the sponge. I'd hate to hear that you had been maimed in any way."

Beth stood very still on the ladder. "I hold life as sacred, Mr Garrett," she said, "I believe God knows what is best for us. No bargains should be made that we cannot keep."

"No bargains made ..." Val snorted, "I wanted that woman so much I said I would give up my dearest treasure to have her."

"And?"

"She didn't come."

"How very distressing for you, Mr Garrett," very softly.

"It might seem silly to you, but ..." Val put a shaky hand to his forehead, "sometimes I feel as though she is thinking of me," then he laughed, "They'll be sending me to a psychiatrist next. Do you think I need one?"

"If you had asked me when I first came, I would have said that you did. Since then I have learned things about you, and I understand better now."

"Thank God for that. I'd hate to think I was going mad."

They laughed together for a moment, and then he asked, "If this man asked you to see him, would you go?"

"Oh yes," Beth answered, "as soon as was humanly possible."

"Would you give up your future career for him?"

"Anything, even my dearest treasure."

"Be careful, in case you are held to that."

"God knows my heart, Mr Garrett, I believe He is making me suffer for the suffering I caused the man I love. If that is so, then I am sure he will give us both our reward."

"If I had any faith left," Val murmured, "I would pray for your happiness in the same breath as I prayed for my own."

Before they could say more, Freddy came striding along the terrace. "Time to meet the train," he said cheerily. "You've interrupted Miss Burke enough for one morning. I'll help you into the car and we can go and pick up Mr Haily. It will be a nice surprise for him, seeing you out and about again."

Val protested. He was enjoying his conversation too much to want to leave. There was no choice, Freddy saw to that, and he wheeled him away.

Beth let out a great sigh of relief. It had only been a very minor repair, and she had wondered just how long she would have to stay up the ladder pretending to be busy.

Now Val had gone she could come down and get herself safely up the stairs and.out of the way where he would not see her when he came home.

Chapter 11

The two neighbours finished shifting the furniture and went home. Rosa wondered in, eager to see how things were progressing. Granny Drummond made a cup of tea and they chatted while they drank it. Then they heard a car drawing up in the drive and Beth remembered things that she had to do upstairs. Rosa followed her but Granny stayed in the hall, looking grim.

The first thing Val did on entering the house was to wheel into his new domain. It was ridiculous to suppose that Miss Burke would still be up the ladder, but he hoped she might have come down to earth and have found something else to do there. He was disappointed. Freddy stood watching him. The change in his patient since Miss Burke's arrival was phenomenal.

Neil was about to follow them into the other room, when Granny Drummond called him back. "I want a word with you, young man," she said, leading the way into the kitchen. Closing the door with a firm click, she turned on their visitor, saying, "I want to know what this 'Betty Burke' nonsense is all about."

"I have no idea what you mean, Mrs Drummond," Neil replied, doing his best to look honest.

"Don't try to be clever with me, Mister Schoolmaster," Granny scolded. "I'm too old for 'clever.' I've seen enough of it in my time, and all too often it leads to trouble. You know very well what I am talking about and I want the truth!"

"Betty has had a falling out with her young man, and I thought …"

"She may well have had a falling out, but if you aren't honest with me, then it will be only a shadow to the falling out we will have. The truth, Mister Schoolmaster, the truth about Betty Burke."

"You know the truth about Betty Burke, Mrs Drummond," Neil replied, his eyes unflinchingly on hers. "I think you know it all."

The old lady nodded. "Aye, perhaps I do." Then, folding her hands very precisely across the front of her apron, she added, "Better you tell me everything, I've guessed the most of it."

"Good, then you will have been careful. I couldn't put it all in a letter for fear Val might see it. I didn't even put her full name."

"Aye, she has always been Miss Burke. When she arrived she told me that her name was Betty. It was quite a surprise I can tell you, Mister *clever* Schoolmaster. More of a surprise because she didn't seem to know the reason for the name herself. That was wrong of you. She should have been told."

"Perhaps it was wrong, but at the time I thought it was best."

"No harm has been done, and a great deal of good. Wise to keep her name from him until he is ready, then he can work it out for himself."

Upstairs Beth was crying softly into Rosa's handkerchief as she told her about the conversation she had had with Val. "The poor dear," she sobbed, "the sacrifice had to be made, *before* the reward was given. He had to give up the thing that was dearest," and she felt cold in spite of the sun at the window.

"Sacrifice?" Rosa asked, wishing she had another handkerchief.

"Yes, sacrifice. Poor Val, the bargain has been kept, and he is too blind to see it."

"What are you talking about?"

Beth quietly told her companion of Val's promise at the village cross. There was an unearthly silence as she finished, and Rosa shuddered.

"That's … creepy," she whispered.

Beth shook her head. "Not really."

"It is to me." Rosa squeezed her friend's shoulders. "Will you be all right? I called in to see Val, there are a couple of letters I want him to read."

"Granny will find her way up soon, I'll manage."

"Good. I'll see you later." Rosa left the room and hurried out onto the landing to find Freddy half way up the stairs coming to meet her. "Hello, Freddy," she called, "Where's that idiot boss of mine?"

"Rosa, my darling," he embraced her, and led her down to the hall. "I did not expect to see you so soon."

"Oh," she shrugged herself away, "I've got some urgent business with Val. Where is the old bear, anyhow?"

"The 'old bear', is right behind you."

Both turned sharply to find Val in the doorway.

"Well, this is progress," Rosa went to him immediately, "Miss Burke warned me that you had moved downstairs, but I didn't expect this. Really, Val, this is the best progress you have made to date!"

"It isn't entirely Miss Burke's fault," Delgado gave the chair a sly push. It was near the metal carpet binder at the door, and he thought that it might cause trouble, "I believe he really wanted to come down all the time, but didn't have the nerve to try. Once she aroused his interest he started getting more adventurous."

"She is very like Beth Riche, I hear," Rosa remarked quietly, "Perhaps that is why Neil sent her."

"Of course, she told me Haily sent her for a particular reason." Now Val was excited, "The more I think of it, the more like Haily it sounds, nasty, underhand, sly," but there was only merriment in his voice, and his eyes sparkled, "That's probably why I never get to seeing the girl. She's luring me out of my hole like a mouse following a piece of cheese. I won't see her until I'm at the bottom of the garden," then with a twirl of his fingers he about faced, and bumped over the metal bar. "You see, Freddy, I can do it, I don't always need a nudge," he crowed.

Evening fell softly on the house and garden. Freddy was taking time off to walk outside with Rosa and Val was relaxing with his friend in his new living space. He had found unexpected pleasure in coming down to ground level and trundling about on the terrace. No one could see him out there, only the few people he trusted, and there was no chance of being stared at.

One thing had upset him, however. Two flights of stone steps had led from the terrace to the lawn. Now there was only one. The second had been converted into a long sloping ramp, which spoilt the view entirely. He glared at his grandmother who was quietly knitting babies clothes. A new baby had been born a few houses down the street from them. In the Highlands a new baby meant new expenses and everyone helped out. Old habits died hard and the knitting needles had come out.

"I can't have it, Granny," he said sharply, "It's got to go."

The old lady made no reply, but perhaps the needles clicked a little more sharply than before.

Neil sighed. "Granny had the steps converted when she first heard that you would be confined to a wheelchair. She didn't think, none of us thought, that you would be content to be stuck in the house for the rest of your life."

"Dammit, Neil, it's almost worth getting on my feet and learning to walk again so that I can have my steps back."

"Why don't you then?"

"I'll not dance again. Crutches will be the best I'll ever manage."

"Do you need to dance?"

"It's all I've got. A life without dancing doesn't seem worth the effort."

"Did you never have a woman in your life?" Neil nodded and smiled slightly, the other man's face was a picture. The furtive glance at his grandmother was priceless. "I mean, did you never have a *particular* woman in your life?"

"Only Rosa."

"Apart from a dancing partner. Val, there must have been someone you wanted to spend the rest of your life with."

"There was … once."

"But?"

"I asked her, and she turned me down."

"I see."

"She had made up her mind, I didn't want to hurt her. I thought too much of her to do that, so I walked away."

"You didn't ask her again, or write, or … anything?"

Val spun away to look out of the window onto the hideous concrete ramp. "I thought it over for a while. Then I had a chance to go back to the village for a visit. I might have asked her again if we had met, but, she had gone. I gave up, and let the weir have me."

"It was Beth, wasn't it."

"Yes." Val sighed. "You're going to lecture me now and call me a fool. I can see it in your face. Go on, I can't stop you. Pace up and down if you like. Melody told me that the children say you always lecture best when you are pacing."

"Do they indeed," Neil stayed firmly in his chair, "I must remember that."

"So? Go on, was I a fool for asking Beth? Everyone knows she's a confirmed spinster, but for some reason she's the one woman for me, and I couldn't think of any other in my life."

Apart from the steady click of the needles, the room was suddenly very quiet. Neil picked a small green thread from the arm of his chair, remnant of that morning's curtain repair. "May I be blunt?" he asked softly.

"Go on."

"I think you were wrong."

"She *is* a confirmed spinster."

"She is now that her one chance has been taken from her. *I meant,* that you were wrong to walk away."

"If I hadn't, it could have turned nasty. I did what was right at the time."

"Yes, and I know that feeling too, though perhaps no one would believe it." Their eyes met and they understood each other without words. A quiet cough from the other side of the room told that Granny had understood as well. Neil continued the conversation with care. "Val, you must understand, Beth is only a spinster because no one has seen beneath the surface. She's no great beauty, like Rosa or Delia ..."

"Or Linda."

"Or, as you say, Linda. They look at her and turn away, unless they want something done. Then oh yes, 'good old Beth' is always there ready and willing to help, grateful for any crumb of kindness."

Val nodded emphatically. "That's true. But I saw the real Beth, the beautiful Beth, when we danced at the Grand Opening. It was in her eyes, they let me see into her soul, and, God Neil, she's exquisite."

"Yes, she is."

"So you've seen it as well."

"I grew up next door to her, if you remember."

"I've got to get over her, Neil. She didn't love me when I had everything to offer, she's not going to love me now."

"How do you know that?"

"I'll be just another sick animal to be pushed around."

"I meant, how did you know she did not love you before?"

"She turned me down."

Neil fixed his eyes on Rosa and Freddy as they walked in the garden. They were an ideal couple. Faced with Rosa as Val's dancing partner he could quite understand Beth's decision. Her adopted parents had been only too ready to tell her, all be it gently, that she was an unattractive child and no man would want her as a wife. It had been a cruel move, but one they had thought kindest. Hard and demanding people themselves, they had not seen the beauty in the sad lonely soul.

"Yes," he replied, "she turned you down because she was brought up to see herself as worthless. All her life she has served, never dreaming of someone serving her. Then suddenly you turned her world on its head."

"I saw her love in her eyes, dammit!"

"The love that would give up what they most desired for the greater good of the man who had proposed ... and stop swearing at me, I won't have it."

"But ... there was no need to give it up."

"Val, you don't want people to see you now because you consider yourself worthless …"

"I am."

"She considered herself worthless when you proposed."

"Oh, don't be …" Neil's stare silenced his words and Val Garrett began to see the world in a different light.

"It is my belief that you two 'worthless people' should get together and defy the world. *We* who know you, know your value. You know she is beautiful, she knows …"

"What?"

"Write to her, ask her to come here and find out for yourself."

Val shook his head and turned away. "I can't," he said hoarsely.

"Damn!" Neil whispered.

A moment of stunned silence and then they both laughed together.

Once more Val turned his attention to the scene in the garden. "If only Freddy was a dancer," he murmured. "Rosa could teach him and he could take my place. She's wasted just running the school."

"He's too heavy." Granny grunted, "Never see him Tango!"

"I wish he could." Val looked up, Rosa had waved to someone at the top of the building across the fence, but he could see nothing.

"I wish Miss Burke had come over to tea. I really must see that girl, she is becoming an enigma, and I don't like it," then his eyes danced with merriment, "Granny, do you think that if I trundled down to the very bottom of the garden, she would come out to talk to me?"

"I wouldn't know," Granny replied not taking her eyes off her stitches.

"Ask Rosa to invite her," Neil advised.

"One day, but first I want the seed catalogue, wherever it is. I'm not having that slide stuck outside my window, it's an eyesore."

"So what are you planning to do," Neil enquired, "make a rock garden of it?"

"No, line it with Cypresses. Freddy says they do wonders with them in Italy."

Chapter 12

Being away from home meant nothing to the schoolmaster. Sunday morning was church morning and he was soon on his way. He had asked Beth to go with him, but fearing that she might be seen now that Val was more mobile, she refused.

Rosa was at the house across the fence but Miss Burke explained that she would prefer to keep Sunday a quiet day with no visits. Once alone she had one thought in mind and mounted the stairs to the top floor. Slowly she drew the curtains. It was like letting light into a shrine. Val's heart was here among the glittering trophies on the shelves and the wardrobe of clothes. She thought of his shoes, and going to the wardrobe cast aside the floating tulle. There was a rack on one side, in which were placed fifteen pairs of finely crafted handmade shoes. She picked up a pair, they looked almost new. In lifting them out, something was knocked from some secret hiding place, and rolled onto the floor at her feet. It was a small dried flower, a Mrs Sinkins pink.

She stooped down, the shoes in one hand, and picked it up. It was exactly the same as the one she had picked in the garden at the Tea Room on the night of the Grand Opening. She smiled and smelt it gently. There was still a trace of perfume left after all that time.

"I thought that I must have dropped it on the way home," she murmured, now realising that it had not been so, and Val had lifted it from the table while she was making the tea.

Even after her refusal the blossom had been one of Val's favourite mascots, and because thoughts of her always seemed to calm him, he took it on every tour to bring luck. Needless to say, he had not thought to take it when he visited the village.

It was late before Beth stirred herself. The shoes were warm when she put them back, for they had been locked in her arms. The dried flower she put carefully in a corner where it would be safe.

Sadly she locked the wardrobe, and turned to close the curtains. For a moment she thought that someone was behind her, and spun about guiltily. No one was there, only her tall slender reflection in one of the mirrors. Yet, somehow it didn't look like the Beth Riche who read newspapers to old ladies and rescued choking swans on the river. She was tall, and slim, her shoulders were square not hunched and her neck long. She had big hands, but linked together as they were, it made them look capable, and not at all ungainly.

For a moment, Beth looked wonderingly into the mirror, was it just the romantic setting, the gilt edging, the windows and the curtains behind her? Or had the knowledge that at least one man had found her attractive, taken away her awkwardness and left in its place if not beauty, then a kind of elegance?

She took two steps forward. There was a poise about her that she had not noticed before.

'Pines are nearer heaven than birches,' Granny had said. Was it true? Was she reaching up like the blue green pines of the forest? Was the love she had for this man filling her and making her forget her old fears?

She knew what her reflection had been before, a slouching, gangling figure, whose deportment was laughable.

Perhaps, she thought, perhaps out there on the dance floor she had forgotten her awkwardness and become sure of her youth and beauty. Was that what Val had seen? She tore herself away, closed the curtains and hurriedly left the room.

"You've been a long time," Rosa remarked, eyeing her suspiciously as she slowly descended the stairs, "I nearly came up to fetch you."

"I'm glad you didn't, or you would have found me either crying my eyes out, or parading in front of a mirror," Beth answered.

"And what were you crying over?"

"A pair of his shoes and a pressed flower. It brought back so many happy memories."

"I suppose we all have to cry sometimes," Rosa rested a sympathetic hand on her arm, "I've cried enough up there since the accident, believe me. Let's hope we are doing all our crying now, and soon the tears will be over."

Someone was whistling 'O Sole Mio' on the other side of the fence. Beth opened the window and looked out. It was Freddy. Back from driving Neil to the station for his return trip to the village, he had taken his patient to inspect the ramp. Val was waving his arms about, and his companion, standing a little to the side and behind him, was enjoying the joke.

"... and I'm not looking out on that for the rest of my life," Val was saying loud enough to be heard, "I've sent for a dozen Cupressus Sempervirens, that should cover the ghastly thing."

"Italian Cypress," Beth called, keeping well in the shadow of the heavy lace curtain. "Good for you, it looks pretty dreadful from up here, too,"

They both looked up, Freddy grinned and nodded, Val trundled a little nearer,

"Hello, Miss Burke. How very nice to see you at last. I always feel that you are hiding from me when you come into the house."

Her heart stopped beating for a moment. Dare she draw aside the curtain and let him see who she really was? She hesitated, it was enough to stop her, "I thought you didn't want to see people," she answered. "Well, that's what I have always been told."

Then a thought came into her head, "I have something to tell you."

"Wonderful! Tell me tonight. Let's have dinner together."

"I'll be too busy. I just want to tell you my news."

"Fire away, then."

She choked and said, "I'm taking your advice, I'm writing to my boyfriend."

"Good luck, don't hurry it. Make sure you put your heart in every word. I hope the fool listens."

"He's not a fool," she couldn't bear to hear him condemn himself, even unknowingly, "He was quite right, I was wrong, but I didn't realise it until now. I do hope it isn't too late."

Freddy murmured something about the evening air being chilly, and there were gnats about. Val was upset, but submitted to being wheeled inside.

Val lingered long after supper that night. His eyes were on the world outside the window, and Freddy wondered what must be going on in his mind.

Hardly a word passed between them, and darkness crept upon the house unnoticed.

In her upstairs room over the fence, Beth sat for a while thinking of what had gone by. Knowing that she could not keep up the pretence much longer, she drew her writing paper towards her, and reluctantly took up her pen. It was difficult to begin, but once started the words seemed to flow so easily. It had all come to her so suddenly. Now she knew that Val had not been entirely blinded by love's lightning, but that she could be straight and proud, as well as careful and caring.

Tonight she must go to bed early, and try to sleep away the dark shadows of her anxiety. Tomorrow she would post the letter. The next day ... She shuddered to think of what might happen the next day, and sealed the envelope before she had a chance to take the letter out and start again.

An hour had passed in silence, when Freddy asked, "What are you thinking?"

Val shrugged and spun about, "Lots of things," he answered, sounding more tired than usual at that time of night.

"Suppose Miss Burke's friend does ask her to come back. You'll be without your cheese. Does that mean the mouse will scuttle back into his hole?"

"I don't think so."

"You, eh, could ask someone else to come."

Val crooked an eyebrow, "Did you have someone in mind?"

Freddy tried to sound casual, "How about Miss Riche?"

For a moment their eyes met, and Val said nothing, then he gave a funny little sigh and turned away, "You know how I feel on that subject."

"Did your conversation with Haily do nothing to change your mind?"

"It helped me understand what had happened, but it's too late now. It wouldn't be fair to try to take it up again after so long. Neil is always right, that's his one fault, but I can't imagine Beth letting my proposal ruin her life. She's too sensible for that. She might have been upset, but she's a clever girl and she will find a way to pick up her life and do what has to be done, regardless."

How blind could a man get? "I'm sure she will find a way." Delgado sighed, it gave him time to control himself, and standing up went over to the window. At that moment he wanted more than anything else to take Val by the lapels and give him the shaking of his life. "Have you thought that for once in her life she might not want to be sensible, that she might be regretting her refusal and be longing for you to ask her again?"

"No, not my Beth. She will go on, head high accepting her destiny."

"Her destiny as an old maid, because you won't swallow your pride and ask her for a second time."

"I can't, not now. She deserves better." Then with a quick smile, "I suppose I must be getting over her."

"Then you've been making a fuss over nothing ..."

The thought made Val was cross. He mumbled something indistinct and wheeled to the fireplace, "It isn't easy to forget a person like Beth," he said gruffly.

"Then why try?"

"Because it's all over. Well, it never really began, did it. She was all I could have loved, and I mean all. Once," and he frowned at the remembrance, "Once she accused me of never looking any further than a woman's face. Being a man yourself you know that's impossible, and I did look at her ankles. But she meant that I didn't look into a person's character. I did with her. I saw such beauty there I was almost dazzled by it. She had everything, grace, charm, warmth. She could love, any fool could see that." His eyes flashed, "Why she hid such a character I shall never know. If she had shown it she would have been married and a mother long ago."

"Perhaps she was waiting for someone to come and awaken the love in her. She might not have wanted to be mother to another man's children."

"Oh what a sight that would be, Beth with a child of her own!"

Freddy let him ramble on, it did good sometimes. Then, when he thought he was at the right pitch he said, "Get her to come and see you. If she does come only out of pity you could always have me throw her out."

"No," Val wheeled over to the other side of the room, "You're not softening me up to it, Freddy, I'll not have her, and that's final."

"You still love her. That's the cause of half your trouble," then with a merciless stab at what might be a sore spot, "Think of it, Beth with your child."

For a moment he wavered, Freddy thought that he had won, but it was not yet time, Val shook his head, "No," he answered indistinctly, "No."

In the morning Beth posted her letter. The people in the area were getting to know her, and she was slowly making friends. Sometimes they asked about Val, but more often it was his grandmother's health they enquired about.

"She needs a young person like yourself to help her with that house," the woman in the post office said, that very morning, "Not that she would agree to have anyone help, so no one here dares to try. If you ask me, that grandson of hers should get married ... then it would take some of the weight off Mrs Drummond's shoulders."

Tuesday dawned, a grey Tuesday, when the world outside took on a soggy, sodden appearance guaranteed to dampen even the brightest of spirits.

Val had awakened in a peculiar frame of mind. He demanded to get up at the crack of dawn, although there didn't seem to be a dawn that day. A roll of thunder in the distance only heightened his spirits.

"Good morning, Granny," he cried as she brought his breakfast things, "I hope you got up early. I did. Freddy is cursing me for raking him out of bed, but I don't care. Look at that rain I'll bet the garden looks better for it. We haven't had decent rain for weeks."

"The rain's so hard you can hardly see the garden through it," Gran contradicted.

"Really?" he wheeled to the window, leaving the breakfast table and looking out over the garden, "With a bit of luck it might wash that concrete away, and I'll have two sets of steps again. Still, it'll make the ground nice and soft for my cypresses."

"I suppose I'll be expected to plant those," Gran grunted, striding over to him and doing her best to bring him back to the table.

Val gave her a little help, "Well, I can't, can I."

"Mr Delgado can do that."

"If he's still here," and Val grinned across the table at his companion who was just finishing his breakfast.

Freddy chuckled over the marmalade, "If you carry on in this frame of mind you won't last the day out, and I'll be leaving in any case."

There was a peculiar grinding noise outside, and Val spun about, "It's my steps," he exclaimed excitedly, then his face fell, "No it isn't, it's only thunder."

"Was he always like this, Mrs Drummond?" Delgado asked, his bright eyes flashing as he watched his companion laying into his meal.

"Sometimes, when the fancy takes him," the old lady sighed.

"I've got ..." Val chewed over a piece of crust, "I've got a peculiar feeling."

"Have it treated, in case it's catching," was Delgado's professional advice.

Val cut him a black look, "You're trying to upset me," he accused.

"Rubbish!" Freddy countered quickly.

Val snorted and pointed threateningly across the table about to make a sharp reply, but his grandmother smacked his hand and told him to eat his food before she took it away.

Cowed for a minute the chatter subsided, and breakfast continued in silence.

Then Val burst out, "I say, I wonder how our Miss Burke is feeling. Her young man will get her letter today. What a brave girl she is. If my fate hung in the balance like that I'd be lost."

"You will be lost if you don't eat your breakfast," Gran scolded, "For I want to clear away."

Val called her something in Gaelic, and enjoyed the look of surprise on her face. "Oh, I can't be serious this morning," he cried. "It's going to be a special day, I've got that feeling."

"Perhaps you had better lie down for a while," Delgado remarked dryly.

"Ah, I might agree with you," Val answered, "but I get these feelings. Ask Granny, ask Rosa, I know when there's something in the air. I generally knew when our performance was going to be a success. I felt it."

Gran glanced up at the sky, "There's only rain in the air today, laddie, and it doesn't look as though it will stop."

"Perhaps it's the cypresses," and Delgado swung casually out of the room.

Chapter 13

Gran busied herself about the house, and once he was left on his own, some of Val's bounce dissolved. Looking out of the wide window onto the soggy garden he faced many facts he had been afraid of before. He was going to become an independent person again, and live his own life. Once he was free he could try to win one of the local girls. He still had his good looks and his money alone would be enough to win some of them. Then he thought of Beth.

Perhaps Neil had been right and she wouldn't find someone else. Suppose she came to see him, suppose ... suppose.

Much to his disappointment, Rosa called round during a break in the rain, with the message that Miss Burke was staying in her room that day. She had been caught out in the rain and she feared that she had started a cold.

The postman always knocked the door with a particular knock when he delivered the letters. Val recognised it at once. Letters were his one contact with the outside world, and he always looked forward to their arrival.

He was a little annoyed with his grandmother for taking them to Freddy first, but he forgave her the moment she appeared with one for him.

Mrs Drummond eyed him warily, and held out the envelope, "Here you are," she said and stood by, waiting.

Val's brow clouded. With a quick flick of his fingers, he ripped open the envelope, the writing was familiar. He flipped to the last page.

"Well?" Gran asked.

Val's face had gone suddenly very white, "Will you leave me to read this on my own, please, Gran?" he said quietly.

Mrs Drummond hesitated. She wanted to be there, to give him a piece of her mind if it were needed. Then she turned and left.

Freddy stopped, one foot on the first stair, "Something wrong?"

"That I can't say," she looked nervously towards the door, "He has her letter. He's thrown me out while he reads it."

"Has he indeed," Freddy brought his foot down, and made towards the back room, but the old lady called him back.

"No, lad," she warned, "it's his life, he must decide for himself what he is going to do with it."

It was half an hour before Freddy finally made his way into the room. He expected Val to have read the letter, and come to his decision. Instead he pulled up sharply as he closed the door.

The rain had abated and a weak sun was once more shining on the garden. Val was by the window, the letter grasped in one great hand, his head bowed onto the other. He did not move as the door clicked shut, but remained perfectly still, and silent.

With steady determination Freddy crossed the room, "I presume that you have had bad news," he said in his briskest, most professional tone. "Can you tell me about it?"

Val's answer was something between a cry and a moan, muffled as it was by his hand it sounded pathetic.

"Have you read your letter?"

There was no reply save a shake of the dark head.

"Are you going to read it?"

"I can't, my head's spinning." He twisted his hand behind him to Delgado. "Here, read it for me."

Freddy looked at the first page, "I can't, Val," he said softly, "it's personal."

"That's why I'm so shaken, you fool," and there was still a little of the early morning banter left in his voice.

"But do you think the lady would mind?"

"For God's sake!" Val spun about. He was mastering the chair more every minute, "I told you to read it."

"If you say so," Delgado took a deep breath and began.

" *'Dear Val,*

I am sending this letter, because I know that I may not be welcome at your house. When you proposed you gave me a little time to consider my answer. I think it is only fair to allow you time to think also.

For the first time in my life, someone had called me beautiful. I thought that you were either deceiving me or yourself.'"

Val turned slowly, so that he faced the darkness of the empty fireplace, a hand covering his features.

Delgado waited his watchful eyes on his patient, the letter he held meant so much to them both, this man and the woman who he had come to respect. He cleared his throat, and continued with difficulty.

"'If only I had trusted you, but I am not as clever as everyone thinks. If I were with you now, I would go down on my knees and beg your forgiveness. I thought that you would soon get over my refusal. Now I know that it is different.

I could not stay in the village, I remembered you at every corner. I went to Wales, but even there I thought of you, and I knew that I wanted to be with you always. It was while I was trying to find the courage to return that I read of your accident. I came back and Neil told me what had happened.

Dear Val, let me come to you and tell you face to face how I feel. At least write to me soon. Tell me to come to you, or go.

Now and for ever,

Your Elizabeth.'"

It was suddenly very quiet, the only sound the crackle of the paper as the Italian folded it, and replaced it in the envelope.

Val held out his hand, and took the letter. His fingers closed firmly round it.

"Are you going to write?" Freddy asked.

Val heaved a sigh, "Later," he replied. "I've got to think what to say, perhaps by tomorrow morning I'll have it straight in my mind."

"You might be able to think better outside, the air will be fresher after the storm."

"No, I'll just …"

Freddy nodded, "If you're going to start brooding again, don't take too long about it. We don't want you slipping back into your shell again."

"I won't. I just want to be on my own for a while … to think."

Wondering what to do for the best, Freddy reluctantly quit the room.

Time and again Val took the letter from its envelope and read it through. Each time he put it carefully back, until at last his eyes were drawn to the postmark. It was a local postmark. The letter had been posted locally. Beth was somewhere in the district. His mind raced. Neil had sent Miss Burke to help Granny with the spring-clean. Miss Burke's voice was uncommonly like Beth's. Her ankles were like Beth's too. When he had seen her standing at the window she had looked like Beth, apart from the hideous bun of hair. Miss Burke had told him that she had fallen out with her boyfriend, and more importantly, that she was writing to him with an apology. Today he had a locally posted letter from Beth.

Oh yes, he felt certain of it now. He had been so wrapped up in his own misfortune that he would never have listened to anyone, even Neil. But Neil understood the way his mind worked, and so he had sent 'Miss Burke' to rescue him from the pit of despair and set his feet on the road to recovery.

He looked down at his feet. Well, it was a nice idea, but he would never get on his feet again, no matter what happened. What had Neil said? 'You two 'worthless people' should get together and defy the world.' Drat the man, he was right again!

Lunch was a subdued and unusually quiet meal. Val was lost in his own thoughts and his companions left him there, hoping that he would find his way to the right conclusions. Rosa called in the afternoon with the news that Miss Burke was feeling much better and had taken herself out into the garden to read a book. One look at Val's face as he spun away from them and trundled out onto the terrace sent her hurrying round the houses so that she would be there for Beth should she be needed.

Val stared at the concrete ramp. It looked dangerous. If he got out of control half way down he could end up on his face in the middle of the lawn. Firm hands gripped the back of his wheelchair.

"If you had said you wanted to come into the garden, I would have helped," Freddy said softly.

"Just down the ramp," Val replied. "If I've got to put up with it, I might as well use the thing."

"Just down the ramp, and I'll leave you on the lawn," Freddy answered.

"Forget the lawn, leave me on the path."

"Certainly."

"Then go back in the house. I want to be on my own. I can't think properly with people about telling me I don't know my own mind."

Going down the ramp was not as unnerving as Val had expected it to be. He would be able to do it himself the next time. Going up it might be difficult, but that bridge would be crossed when he came to it and not before.

The path was not as easy to wheel on as carpets. It was cursed several times before Val reached the bottom of the garden and the fence between the two properties.

Beth had taken her book into the garden that fresh afternoon, not to read, but to plan her next move. For a long time she had stood on the terrace. It was a lovely scene, and one she wanted to remember if she was sent away. Before her the gardens stretched in a tidy disorder, which made broad sweeps in the lawns, and long grass in clumps under the trees.

At the end of the path lay a small orchard. They would have a bumper crop this year, Granny had said. Smiling she settled down on the little rustic seat by the apple trees.

Deep in her thoughts she did not hear the crunch of gravel as Val approached. His voice coming from the other side of the fence startled her.

"Mr Garrett!" she cried. "You made me jump."

"Sorry." He wanted to shout out, 'I know who you are,' but now was a time for patience. He had not been patient before. This time there must be no mistakes. "Did you write to your boyfriend?" he asked, already sure that he knew the answer.

There was a little pause before she said, "Yes."

"Was your letter well received?"

"He hasn't had time to reply yet."

"I think he has," very quietly, then louder, "Are you looking forward to his letter?"

"No."

"No?" What the devil was going on her strange female mind, he wondered.

"I am afraid."

"Afraid?"

"I've been deceiving him, he didn't know I came here ... he ... I mean..."

"I think he knows, Miss Burke. He knows and he will be eternally grateful."

"I'm afraid I don't understand what you are saying, Mr Garrett."

Val sighed. Stalemate, they could go no further. "You haven't told me your first name," he said, the glimmering of an idea taking shape in his mind.

"There was really no need," Beth replied. Neil had warned her to stay formal with him, it had all been a part of his plan.

"Please, Miss Burke, I would like to know."

"It's Betty, sir." Beth frowned at the sudden burst of laughter from the other side of the fence. "Something is wrong with that, Mr Garrett?"

"The devious little swine, *just wait till I get my hands on him!*" Val glanced up. A lilac tree was growing hard against the fence, its branches thick enough and just within reach. There may be no use in his legs, but his hands and arms were still strong. Gritting his teeth he gripped the lowest branch and hauled himself onto his feet. The wheelchair wobbled and fell over with a clatter as he left it. He glanced down at it. That was going to be a problem. Then again, if he was right it was probably a problem soon to be overcome. Then he looked over the fence. There she was, the mysterious Betty Burke, only not so mysterious now. "Hello, Beth," he said.

She spun about and looked up at him, her lips trembling and her eyes swimming in tears, "Forgive me, please forgive me," she whispered, "I have done this to you. I should have trusted you in the beginning."

"Oh, Beth," his words were softer, but no louder than a sigh, "The blame is mine, I made a pact with God, but I was too impatient. I expected my prayer to be answered at once. I should have known it would take time."

"Then you have your faith restored?"

"How can I doubt His mercy, I said I would give up my dearest treasure if I could have you. My career is gone, but you are here. God kept His bargain, despite my disbelief."

"He also sent an angel to guide us. I don't agree with what you called Neil a moment ago."

Val hung onto his branch grinning smugly. "You would if you knew," he replied.

"Knew what?"

"He was giving us a clue. I would have known, that was why you were always Miss Burke to me. Granny would know … I wonder if she does?"

"But I don't, and I think as I'm rather involved I should be told." Beth turned and knelt on the seat to face him over the fence.

"Betty Burke, the lady who was not what she seemed."

"I still don't understand."

"When the Young Pretender was escaping the Redcoats he dressed as a serving maid and called himself Betty Burke. The name saved his skin, and it's probably saved ours too."

"Oh, as you say, devious and little, but I won't agree with the rest, I think I like angel better."

"You would. *All the ladies* see Neil Haily as an angel." Then he frowned. "Beth, can you come round, rather quickly if you don't mind. Sprint round the houses, I know you can run, they told me that you can cover the ground at a fair old speed when needed."

"Am I needed so urgently?"

"I'm afraid so. You see, when I pulled myself up, I knocked my chair over … and

I'm not used to being on my feet ... and the world is beginning to spin. If I fall ... I'll damage the shrubbery and Granny ..."

The next instant Beth had executed a brilliant gate vault over the fence and was righting his wheelchair. Grimly she shoved it under him and lent a ready shoulder as he levered himself back down to safety.

Freddy had been watching the scene from the window. When Val knocked over his chair he had been about to dash out into the garden to help him but Granny held him back.

"Let them sort it out for themselves," she advised.

Beth's leap over the fence drew a gasp of admiration from the Italian, but Granny only nodded and smiled. She had taken a strong liking to the girl, even before Neil had confirmed her suspicions as to who she really was. If anyone was going to get her grandson back on his feet, this was the young lady to do it, she thought.

"Perhaps we should leave them to themselves for a while," she murmured. "They will have a lot to discuss. If they are not back in the house in time for dinner, then you might perhaps go down and fetch them."

Delgado nodded and reluctantly left the window.

Dusk descended softly on the garden.

Under the trees Val sat perfectly at peace with the world, Beth's head in his lap. Neither spoke. All that had needed to be said had been said, words seemed inadequate things now.

"We've been a couple of fools, haven't we," he said at last, his hand resting on her head.

"I suppose so," she wiped away her tears, happy tears, with long strong fingers. How glad she was of those big hands. Their strength would be needed now, "I doubted you from the very beginning."

"Not without cause." He ran his fingers through her hair, he could do that now the bun was no longer there. It was beautiful hair soft and fine, made for touching. "I came too suddenly, I can see that now."

"I was trying to make myself into something I'm not." She smiled sadly thinking of the past. "I might be strong and capable in a crisis …"

"You were when you came over the fence. Even I didn't expect that of you!"

"… but inside there has always been a sad little 'me' crying out to be loved."

"You didn't fool me though, I saw what you were really like. I knew, and you'll get that love. I promise you."

She sighed contentedly, knowing that he told the truth. "I wish I had believe you, but it seemed so impossible at the time."

He hugged her, "But you believe me now."

"Yes, now I do."

"Good. It's getting late, and it must be nearing dinner time. If we don't go back to the house soon, Granny will come down and start scolding us."

"Oh, Val!"

"In any case, we are probably keeping the fairies awake. We are at the bottom of the garden you know … Take me back to the house."

For the first time they all had dinner together, Granny presiding over her table with the air of a Duchess in the grandest mansion. Her stern old heart filled with joy that the two young couples had found happiness in her home. Memories of her own dear husband filled her mind. She knew what it was like to love and be loved. Ephraim Drummond had been a kind and caring man. She smiled at his memory. Yes, she had known true love.

The meal over the young couples went their own ways. Rosa took the long road round the houses, vowing all the while that if no one made a gate in the fence soon, she would punch a hole in it herself. Slipping into bed that night she hugged her pillows and fell contentedly asleep to dream of future happiness.

Over the annoying fence Freddy and Granny kept well out of the way.

Val and Beth sat by the big window in the quiet calm of his room watching the stars, while in the distance a bird sang a glorious hymn to the moon. What they said no one save themselves knew.

The change in the man was phenomenal. With her aid, Val was now seated in one of the large arm chairs. For the first time since the accident he had changed from his ordinary clothes and shone once more resplendent in dinner jacket and handmade shoes, clothes which he had once been so used to and thought never to wear again. His road to recovery had begun.

The End